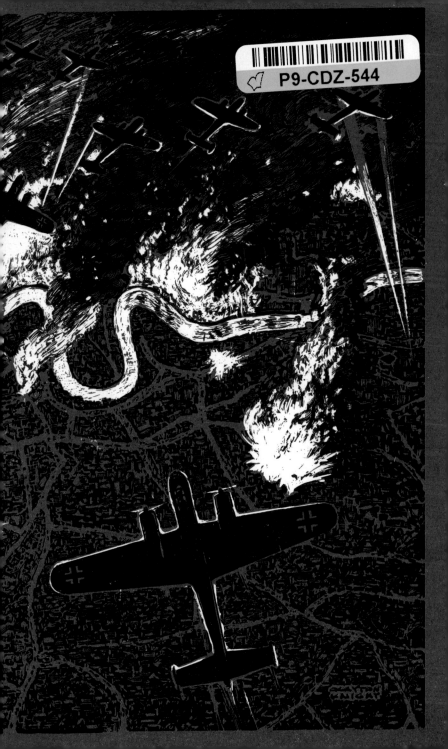

WE WERE THERE

AT THE

Battle of Britain

Another ship went spinning down in flames

WE WERE THERE

AT THE

Battle of Britain

By CLAYTON *and* K. S. KNIGHT

Historical Consultant:
THE DUKE OF HAMILTON, K.T.

Illustrated by CLAYTON KNIGHT

Publishers GROSSET & DUNLAP *New York*

PRINTED IN THE UNITED STATES OF AMERICA
LIBRARY OF CONGRESS CATALOG CARD NO. 59-12010

We Were There at the Battle of Britain

In August of 1940,
while the Royal Air Force was battling heroically
in the skies over the British Isles,
Winston Churchill, Prime Minister
of Great Britain, told his people:
*"Never in the field of human conflict was so much
owed by so many to so few."*

Contents

CHAPTER

I	The War Comes to Holmewood	3
II	The Dog Gets a Name	17
III	Where Is Alan?	29
IV	The Channel Shores	37
V	The Ordeal at Dunkirk	48
VI	England Awaits the Invasion	73
VII	Alan Sees the London Docks	88
VIII	The Beginning of the Blitz	104
IX	Peter Joins Churchill's "Few"	123
X	Oklahoma Bound	137
XI	A Moment of History	150
XII	The Luftwaffe Admits Defeat	169

Illustrations

Another ship went spinning down in flames
                                  Frontispiece

"Quiet down, Sireen," he said coaxingly   18

The Allies had opened sluice gates near
    Gravelines   35

For all Alan's care, the two craft met with a
    jarring thump   68

Operation Dynamo had about completed
    its mission   71

They had to learn to endure one wartime
    disaster after another   78

"That's our ship," Bart said   90

"Stop yer bawlin' now, duckie," she crooned
    hoarsely   97

"We licked them dunderheads once, and no
    reason we won't lick 'em again."   120

WE WERE THERE
AT THE
Battle of Britain

CHAPTER ONE

The War Comes to Holmewood

THE down-train from London was due at the small Sussex village of Middle Pentworth early in the evening. But since World War II had started, the train was often late.

Alan Lyons and his ten-year-old sister Cicely waited for their father and his overseas guest on the platform of the smoke-stained brick station. Cicely said, "What do you think Daddy's American will be like, Alan? Is a person from Oklahoma an Indian?"

Her brother, a slim boy of fourteen with a thick mop of light-brown hair and lively blue eyes, laughed. "Of course not, silly. Mr. Gordon just lives in the state of Oklahoma." Alan was being kept busy holding on to the leash of a nondescript dog whose coat showed signs of having been recently scrubbed. The animal watched the children nervously and squirmed at any sudden noise.

The air was soft and warm as it often is in England in May. Except for the earlier unexpected appearance of the dog in the garden of the Lyons' home, the day in sleepy Middle Pentworth had passed with no usual event—even though the British Government had declared war against Germany on September 3, 1939, eight months earlier. Since then, everyone had talked as though Hitler and his Nazi armies might start trouble on English soil at any time.

In every British home, people listened with sober faces to the evening radio news telling about the slaughter of Poland by the Nazis. Alan read these reports in the newspapers, discussed them with his father and in some of his classes in school. But like most of the people of Britain during the winter of 1939–40, Alan and Cicely watched the war preparations in the village with annoyance.

Trenches had been dug right across the town park, spoiling the cricket field. And ugly walls of sandbags were now piled against the police station and the quaint little town hall.

Across the windows of every house and building

in Britain hung thick black-out curtains, so that no light should be seen by night-flying German planes seeking a target. And hallways everywhere were littered with stirrup pumps and pails of sand for putting out fires from bomb strikes.

On September 4th, the children's older brother Peter had announced that he was leaving school to join the Royal Air Force to train as a pilot.

Accepted quickly, Peter had soon been posted to a Flying Training School. Here he learned about radio, engines, air navigation and, after some weeks, the business of handling an aircraft in flight under the critical eye of an instructor who often barked at him, "Lyons, you *must* learn never to . . ." or "Tomorrow we practice acrobatics again."

Finally Peter had reached the glorious moment when he was allowed to fly solo—alone, with no check pilot in the plane. However, he still had several months of training ahead before he would be able to master the more complicated tricks of air fighting.

After Hitler destroyed Poland, everyone believed that he would send an invasion army against Britain and that Nazi bombs would blast the British Isles. So, all that winter, concrete road blocks against German tanks were installed on all roads leading from the sea.

David Lyons, the children's father, went out as air-watch warden after he came home from his work in a London publishing firm, whenever an alarm was sounded.

Though most of Britain had been quiet that winter, there was frequent heavy firing down by the English Channel. The grumbling noise often wakened Alan very late, and he would lie listening, remembering bits of conversation he had heard. And when his father came softly upstairs after his hours of late warden duty, the boy would call, "What's going on, Dad? Are the Germans coming?" And his father would whisper, "Oh, no, it may be the Nazis are laying mines outside our harbors. Pop off to sleep now. . . ."

But the country lanes and hills around them were quiet and, with the melting of the last snow of winter, spring flooded Sussex with calm, sweet winds and the fragrance of new grass.

Then, on the 9th of a bright, cheerful April, Middle Pentworth and all Britain had been jolted out of this period of brooding quiet. The Lyons family listened to the radio news that the Nazis had that morning staged a fearful assault on Norway and Denmark, exactly as they had on Poland. The

British War Office announced that Britain was going to the rescue of her ally, Norway.

As he listened, Mr. Lyons signed and said, "Pity, we haven't enough men or guns to do much good. We can't strip our own country of all our defences even to save Norway, much as we'd like to." And all over Britain, people listening to the news said, "If Hitler means to attack one small country after another, where will he stop?"

In the family library Alan and Cicely were following the march of the German forces on a map. Surrounding the map were photographs of Hitler, Goering, Rudolf Hess, and other German generals and admirals—England's enemies. One day Alan drew a red line through conquered Norway, as he had through Poland.

A month after that, Britons learned that the Nazi Juggernaut had rolled again, this time into Holland, Belgium, and Luxembourg. Alan wondered whether he would soon have to use his red pencil on them, too.

Brushing aside her long fair hair, and peering at the map over his shoulder, Cicely stared with wide eyes. "Why, Alan!" she said, "those countries are right across the Channel from England. That brings the Germans awfully close to us, doesn't it?"

"Of course it does," Alan replied. "But what

d'you think Peter's gone into the RAF for? He's learning how to fly so he can stop the Germans if they try to land in England."

"Oh," Cicely smiled comfortably, "that's all right then. He won't let them land."

"Of course he won't," Alan snorted.

But the older people of Middle Pentworth were not quite so sure everything was all right with England.

Officer Bottley, sergeant of the police of Middle Pentworth, said to a worried neighbor, "We've got Churchill running the war now, and 'e'll let 'Itler know wot's wot soon enough." Then turning to a passing youth, he said sharply, "Where's yer gas mask, sonny? Never leave it 'ome. Run along and get it, there's a spry lad."

Mrs. Plume, a plump, middle-aged woman who bustled into the Lyons' home once a week to help with the cleaning, held strong opinions about the situation. She announced to Mrs. Lyons one day: "Mister Winnie Churchill tells us 'e's got noffink to offer us but blood, toil, tears, and sweat. Lumme, that's a small price to pay, for a Henglishman defending 'is 'ome. Sweat and tears we've got any'ow —who wouldn't add a bit o' blood to keep them Nazis out?"

Things were moving fast. On May 14th, Rotterdam, in Holland, had been all but destroyed. Then the Nazis raged swiftly into Belgium and France,

and now Englishmen knew that the best of their troops—the British Expeditionary Forces—and most of the war equipment Britain had were there on foreign soil. If they were lost, Britain would have little to defend herself with.

But on the evening when Cicely and Alan went down to the station to meet the American guest, Bartley Gordon, and their father, the odd arrival

[*9*]

of the dog was the thing they were most interested in.

When the train's shrill high-pitched whistle warned of its approach, the dog, which Alan was trying to hold in a firm grip, began to tremble and whine in spite of Cicely's efforts to quiet him.

Alan watched the dog anxiously. "Try to calm him down, Sis," he urged. "If Dad thinks he's nervous and excitable he'll never let us keep him."

The train slid quietly into the station, the side doors—customary on English trains—flew open along its length, and passengers crowded onto the platform. Alan soon caught sight of his father with his American friend striding along beside him.

The children stared curiously at their visitor as he approached. Shorter than their lean father by half a head, his ruddy face was crowned by a wide-brimmed light gray hat with a narrow ribbon band —like the hats they had seen in Western movies. So this was Bartley Gordon from the funny place called Oklahoma!

Cicely flung herself into her father's arms while the American grinned over Mr. Lyons' shoulder at the boy and dog.

"Well, now, this must be Alan," he said. "Glad to see you, boy." Bartley Gordon thrust out a hand, and then halted with a surprised "Well,

what's this?" A switch engine in the railway yards
had whistled shrilly, and the dog made a lunge between his legs. Backing and twisting excitedly, the
animal managed to tighten the leash around both
of the men's ankles in spite of Cicely's frantic efforts to untangle them.

The Oklahoman glanced down calmly. "Now,"
he said, "that's what I call a warm welcome. What's
his name?" He reached down, slipped the leash
from the dog's collar, and swept him up into the
crook of a big arm.

Alan said, "He hasn't a name yet, sir."

Bartley Gordon put his hand on Cicely's head.
"And this pretty little blonde is Cicely, I bet," he
said.

David Lyons answered hastily, "Sorry, Bart. My
daughter Cicely. But I must confess I don't know
whom that dog belongs to." He turned a severe
frown on Alan, who broke out, "Can we keep
him, Dad? He's a war orphan, I think." And Cicely
cried, "Please, Daddy."

"We'll see later," their father said. "This way,
Bart." And aside to Alan, "Put that dog's leash on,
son, and make him behave!"

The ten-minute walk through the tranquil English village to Holmewood, the Lyons' place, gave
Alan and Cicely a chance to point out to their

visitor the air-raid shelters, the town cricket field, and the sandbagged police headquarters on the cobbled village square.

Long before this meeting, the two children had begun to feel that they already knew Bartley Gordon well. Their father had told them many stories about himself and the American. The two men had been fliers together in the first World War. Over the years the acquaintance had been kept up warmly, and now here was Gordon himself. He had come to London a few weeks earlier as a representative of an American aircraft-engine builder to talk to the British Air Ministry about their needs. Tonight he had arrived to get better acquainted with the entire Lyons family.

When they stopped at the entrance to the Lyons' house and garden, he exclaimed, "So this is Holmewood!"

Mr. Lyons opened the gate, and the dog, leash flying, bounded up the brick path between thick rows of tulips with the children following.

Bartley Gordon grinned at the sight. Then, catching a view of the house with its mellowed old walls, its mossy slate roof and casement windows, he stopped in frank admiration.

"Dave," he exclaimed, "this is a wonderful spot! Why, I don't think there's a place like it in all Oklahoma. But I wish it were somewhere else," he added seriously. "This village is right spang in the front line in this war. Tell you what—let me see if I can't convince your wife that she should take the kids and go to the States. We'd like 'em to stay at our place till this mess is over."

Before Mr. Lyons could reply, the children brought their mother out to welcome their guest.

Shortly thereafter, Mrs. Lyons led them to a great oak table in the low-ceilinged dining room. "If we have dinner right away we'll have time afterward for a sit in the garden until we have to 'black out,'" she explained.

When the last spoonful of dessert had been

swallowed, Mrs. Plume, who had come over "to lend a 'and with dinner," cheerfully ordered everyone out to the terrace. "You 'ave your coffee there, so's I can tidy up a bit and get meself 'ome in case the sireens go."

Twilight was settling when she bustled off, and the soft flower-laden air enfolded them in a disarming peace. The dog lay still on the grass, his head on his paws, his brown eyes turning trustfully from one child to the other.

"Now, Alan," his father asked, "how does this animal happen to be here in the first place?"

"I don't know how he *got* here," Alan began, and Cicely added, "We found him hiding in Mother's delphiniums. And he was so dirty and scared—"

Mrs. Lyons interrupted. "When Alan and Cicely discovered him, I wanted to ask Sergeant Bottley to come and remove the poor thing, but the children wouldn't hear of it. He seemed friendly and glad to be rescued, and he came out when the children called. So the next thing I knew, I found myself helping the children give him a bath. He didn't seem to be hurt, only frightened. He ate as if he were half starved."

"Of course he did," Mr. Lyons exclaimed. "And

that's one point. It's all we're going to be able to do just to feed this family on war rations. Chances are, food will get even scarcer. Besides, if he's so friendly, he's probably somebody's pet."

"But Dad," Alan broke in, "I'll give him part of my rations, and so'll Cicely. And we *promise* to give him back if we find out he belongs to somebody else."

Bart, who had been listening in amusement, decided to put in a word. "This fellow looks to me like a good ratter. Got one of that breed—if you call it a breed—at home."

By this time Mr. Lyons reluctantly felt himself softening toward the dog.

"The cards are stacked against you, Dave," Bart Gordon laughed. "You'd better make up your mind to let them keep him."

With the failing light the bats came out and darted in crazy angles overhead. The scent of spring flowers saturated the air. The creak of a lawn chair punctuated the conversation. And dully and from far away, toward Dover, came the sound of guns like the rumble of trucks crossing a wooden bridge.

A few pencil-thin searchlights shot up into the darkening clouds from the area of London, swung nervously in wide arcs, paused momentarily, fitfully disappeared, and flared upward again.

Mrs. Lyons motioned to the children that it was time for bed.

Alan and Cicely, followed by the waggling dog, started for the house.

Suddenly, from the south, came the rising wail of a siren. And the mournful sound was soon joined from other points, till the air was filled with the eerie rise and fall of the chilling chorus.

CHAPTER TWO

The Dog Gets a Name

AT THE first wail the dog leaped wildly, and set up a throaty rising and falling din that matched the sirens in dismalness. Even Alan's soothing and Cicely's petting failed to stop his yelps or trembling.

Mr. Lyons said hastily, "I'd better get over to the Warden's Center about this warning. Alan, *please quiet that dog.*"

Bart was already on his feet. "Alan," he said, "I think I've got a name for that fellow. What d'you think of *Sireen?* Fits him, doesn't it?" Then he turned to catch up with his host. "Wait, Dave," he called, "no harm if I tag along, is there? I must learn the ropes."

Mr. Lyons beckoned him on.

"Quiet down, Sireen," he said coaxingly

Back on the terrace, Alan looked down at the dog. "Quiet down now, Sireen," he said coaxingly.

The animal looked up, and slowly his wails ceased, and his tail began to wag furiously.

"Shall we go to bed now, Sireen?" the boy suggested encouragingly. Much to his surprise the pup lurched to his feet, slowly his hackles smoothed, and he followed the children upstairs.

The two men threaded their way at a good gait through the black streets to the square. They caught up with Sergeant Bottley just as he was entering the station through the thick black-out curtains at the door. Inside the brightly lighted room were other wardens, and a deputy policeman was at a desk, speaking into the phone.

"Jerry's attacking our coast defences tonight," the policeman reported, putting down the receiver.

Bottley went into the Alert routine, sending out patrols in pairs to make sure no lights were showing in the town. As volunteer workers arrived he gave them their assignments, and the closely shuttered room became hot and stuffy. Neighbor greeted neighbor, some grim, others joking.

Alf Whitty, a square, clumping man in well-worn corduroys who owned a lorry and did carting jobs, stopped to chat with Mr. Lyons and his friend from America. "I 'ope they don't 'ave it as rough down Portsmouth way as it was when I drove there last night," he said, shaking his helmeted head. "Some o' them ruddy Nazi bombers come over the Channel, and they caught me on the road near Emsworth village. They give me a nasty few minutes in a ditch till they dumped their loads. Didn't 'it the airfield, but they made a shockin' mess of some nice little 'omes in Emsworth."

He paused to light his pipe and continued, "I 'elped to dig out a few o' the folks got buried. We 'ad to work fast when some buildings caught fire, but it 'ad started to ryne 'ard by then, and that 'elped put out the fires. We pried out a young couple and their little dog buried under a clutter o' roof tiles and beams, but blimey if their pup didn't go streakin' off the minute we got 'im loose, makin' a noise like a sireen." Whitty sighed noisily. "We got that couple into the 'orspital, though."

Mr. Lyons exchanged glances with Bart Gordon. "Emsworth village is only ten miles away from here. Does Alan's dog look as though he could run that far?" he asked, and Bart replied, "Could be."

Since no German planes seemed to be coming inland that night, a couple of wardens started a dart game, and presently the "All Clear" sounded.

Sergeant Bottley announced, "Well, men, that's all fer t'night—I 'ope. Off with yer now, and thanks."

Mr. Lyons and Bart Gordon went out into the warm darkness. Hundreds of searchlights still stabbed into the dark clouds as they walked home. A few minutes later they found Mrs. Lyons waiting for them in the pleasant, book-lined study.

"Well, no great harm done tonight, apparently," she said cheerfully.

"No," said Bart. "But listen, folks," he went on earnestly. "Your village isn't going to be safe for long. And my wife and I can't bear the idea of you and the kids staying here so near the Channel. There are airfields all around which the Nazis are going to blast. You might just as well come over and stay with us. We have a big ranch near Tulsa, a horse Alan can ride, and two, three ponies I bet Cicely'd love."

The clock ticked unusually loud for a moment.

Mrs. Lyons smiled. "You're awfully kind, Bart," she said. "And I suppose you're right. But there are so many things to think about—the family separated, and there's no possibility of my leaving David or Peter now." She looked up at her husband. "What do you think, David?"

Mr. Lyons managed to say matter-of-factly,

"Well, I'm not sure the children would be allowed to leave. You *are* kind to offer, Bart, but—"

Bart Gordon rose and leaned against the mantel. "Listen," he said soberly. "A friend of mine in Air Intelligence told me that when the Germans bombed Rotterdam they leveled it to the ground—flat. Everything! Now their bombers are wiping out Belgium and France. Do you think the French can stop them? Can anybody, with the limited troops and equipment the Allies have against that big German war build-up? So, what happens when France falls and the Nazi armies are just across the Channel from this village?"

Mr. Lyons interrupted tartly, "Aren't you over-looking the fact, Bart, that the English always *have* managed somehow, when their backs were against the wall? We'll muddle through. No enemy since the Normans has licked us yet."

"Look, Dave," Bart exploded. *"Sure,* you muddle through, and you've got the best planes and the best airmen. But face it, you haven't got *enough,* as yet. Do you think Hitler's going to wait?"

After a pause to catch his breath, he went on. "Meanwhile the British Expeditionary Force is across in France, and they're being boxed in on two fronts by those Nazi Panzer columns right this minute. Who can be sure they'll ever get out?"

Mr. Lyons shook his head obstinately. "I only know Britain'll manage to defend herself, Bart. We always have."

"Whew," sighed the American, and wiped his forehead impatiently. "Well, *think* about it. I've got some pull with the shipping people. Let me try to arrange passage on some ship for the children, at least, in case you do decide to let us take care of them."

Alan saw to it that he got downstairs next morning in time to accompany his father and the American to the train.

As they moved along through the slanting morning sunlight, Gordon asked, "How'd you like to see Oklahoma, son?"

"You mean we'd all go to America, Mr. Gordon?" Alan asked eagerly.

"Well, no, I guess not all of you," Bart said. "Occurred to me you and Cicely might like to spend some time over there with our kids—you know, riding horses—"

"Would there be any red Indians?" Alan asked.

Bart laughed. "Lots of 'em, but not the movie kind. One of my foremen on the ranch is a full-blooded Choctaw. His grandfather was a ripsnortin' fighter, but our Indian's the gentlest, mildest old coot on the place. Teach you to ride Western style, probably."

Alan laughed. "It sounds wonderful, Mr. Gordon."

The good-bys at the train were hasty, but Bart shouted that he'd be back again soon.

Alan was a good student, but somehow he found his mind roving a bit among red Indians that day. During an afternoon class his schoolmaster, Mr. Smollett, peered at him sharply over his glasses and rapped, "Lyons, do I have your attention? Well, then . . ."

It was a draggy sort of day, and the entire roomful of pupils seemed to be half asleep, in spite of Mr. Smollett's tapping finger, when again the mournful wail of a siren disturbed the warm stillness. Instantly teachers and children rose to form lines in the march to the trenches dug in the schoolyard. Outside, Alan quickly noticed the erratic vapor trails of three aircraft against the sky, tracing the crazy pattern of a dog-fight that was sweeping toward them high overhead. There was the sound of gun-fire as Alan and his friend, Rod Small, scrambled into a corner of the trench from which they could keep a wide part of the sky in view.

There was the giggle of the littler girls, and the crunch of gravel as the schoolmasters hurried around to make sure the children were all tucked down safely below ground level.

Above, the planes darted like distant dragon-flies, almost playfully. The spectacle brought no sense of danger to the children. The teachers, dismayed by their antics, called sternly, "No nonsense in the trench, children. You older boys, Gregory, Lyons, Small—keep order there."

Alan looked up and saw that the swirling planes were approaching swiftly, growing larger with each second.

Just at that instant one plane, pursued by the other two spitting fire, swooped down to tree-top level in a vast circle, and Mr. Smollett leaped into the trench. The leading plane, shuddering, began a rapid climb straight up. Alan shouted, "It's a JU-87. A Stuka. See the black Nazi crosses!" and Rod Small cried, "Will you look at those Hurricanes going after it!"

The RAF fighters roared down, guns blazing, and the little girls gasped. A teacher cried, "Stay down flat, *everybody!*" And a branch clipped from a tree floated gently into the trench. Rod reached out to grasp it, not taking his eyes from the planes.

The noisy sky-battle was over quickly. A quarter of a mile away, and not much more than five hundred feet above the schoolyard level, the German plane, trailing black smoke, staggered drunkenly upward in a puff of flame, turned on its back, and went into a rolling plunge.

As flames licked along its wings Mr. Smollett shouted, "Arms over your heads, everybody, and *stay down!*" The words were barely out when the Junkers crashed, making the ground tremble.

The boys popped their heads up. "There's one of the crew," Alan whispered. He pointed out a long ribbon of white fluttering against the cloud and the blossoming of a parachute that danced along, swinging and turning slowly as it descended.

The children saw a dense column of black smoke rising from a field nearby. The parachute with its dangling passenger was twisting down a little farther off.

After the jubilant Hurricane pilots made a sweeping pass overhead, it was not long before the village "All Clear" sounded. Mr. Smollett dusted himself off and said, "Close call, that." Then he led the youngsters back to the classrooms.

On the way, Alan said to his friend, "Hang onto that tree branch, Rod. Maybe we can find some more souvenirs where that Stuka crashed."

But this hope was never fulfilled since the police lost no time roping off the area around the crashed enemy plane until RAF Intelligence officers could arrive to inspect it.

Later, as Alan and Cicely were hurrying home after school, Alan suddenly exclaimed, "Cicely! What do you suppose happened to Sireen while all that racket was going on?"

"Oh!" cried Cicely. "Come on, let's run!" They pelted into Holmewood to find their mother searching the shrubbery. She stood up when she saw them and cried, "Thank heaven, you two are home, but I'm awfully afraid, children, that Sireen's gone."

CHAPTER THREE

Where Is Alan?

Ever since Alan questioned his American friend about Oklahoma, he and Rod had been talking about Indians a good deal. The subject had stirred up rather heated arguments between the boys. Bart Gordon's description of present day Indian tribes didn't fit in with what Rod had seen in the movies. Since Alan and Cicely visited the cinema a good deal less than he did, Rod felt he ought to be considered the expert.

"How could they make all those moving pictures if there weren't Indians in feathers and war paint all around?" Rod insisted.

"You think Mr. Gordon doesn't know?" Alan retorted crossly. "Well, he ought to. He lives there."

The dispute over the Indians rankled, and Rod developed a chip on his shoulder, although formerly the two boys had done everything together cheerfully. But the loss of Sireen was something different. Partly because he loved his own old family St. Bernard, Rod could sympathize with the way Alan and Cicely felt about the puppy they had adopted.

It turned out that the postman had probably noticed the dog during the air battle, bolting off toward the opposite side of town. A similar dog had run into a grocery boy's bike about the time the "All Clear" sounded. But after that—blank.

Although the children went on with their own affairs, after Sireen's disappearance life in Middle Pentworth slowly became muddled by the state of war. Mr. Lyons now often found himself, like many Englishmen, unsure of whether he'd be able to complete things he set out to do.

He had planned to make a trip to Ireland for his publishing firm toward the end of May to consult with an Irish author. Mr. Lyons had always looked forward to those Dublin visits. Now, however, he was uneasy about going away from home because of the darkening war news.

There was no doubt that Hitler's plan to conquer Europe was coming dangerously close to success. The French and the English had been gallantly inflicting heavy losses on the Germans. But, only that week, the Nazi Panzer columns had begun to cut them off from escape by sea. And the Germans, taking the French Channel ports of Calais and Boulogne, had now nearly closed the loop around the B.E.F. A collapse in France would free Hitler to turn his wrath on Britain.

One evening toward the end of May, Bart Gordon phoned. Alan and Cicely heard their father say, "Yes, we heard the news broadcast tonight. Things in France couldn't look much worse. We had a Nazi plane shot down right over our own village this week and Sireen bolted . . . no word about him at all."

After a long pause, Mr. Lyons said, "You think you may have arranged passage for the children? Yes, Grace and I have about decided it *is* better for them to get over to America if they can. Call me as soon as you know."

Mrs. Lyons had planned that the children should have new clothes for the trip. Most of them could be found nearby, except that Alan needed shoes that had always been bought from a shop in London.

Naturally, Alan had begun to feel a growing excitement about the proposed trip to America. He decided to go down to the family cottage at the seaside as soon as he could, and gather up some possessions he wanted to take with him. When he asked Rod to go along, the other boy said, "Are you sure your parents'll let you do that?" And Alan retorted rather uncertainly, "Well, I don't know as they'd exactly *let* me go if I asked them, but they'll think it's a good idea when I get back. How about next Saturday?"

"I'll try," Rod replied.

On the night of the 23rd of May, Alan sat beside the radio with the family. The cool, quiet voice of the announcer told them that the Belgian and French armies were now making a last heroic stand around the towns of Menin and Ypres.

"And worst of all," Mr. Lyons said at the end

of the harrowing broadcast, "there's a rumor that the King of the Belgians may make a separate peace. This would mean nearly half a million Belgian soldiers taken out of action. If they are, I hate to think what will happen to the rest of the Allies." He sighed.

"It looks bad. But my company thinks I can get over to Dublin and back before anything can happen here. They say I'd better go while I can."

And so, on the afternoon of the 31st, David Lyons left for Ireland. It was a long, dreary train ride up to Holyhead where he took the night boat for Dublin. The people in the train were grimly buried in their newspapers and still grimmer thoughts.

On Monday night, Mr. Lyons returned by boat and train to London. Arriving at Euston Station in the morning, he stopped to have breakfast on his way to the office. When he unfolded his newspaper he discovered that while he had been away, history had been rolling to a great climax. The shocking headlines told him that the worst had happened:

"OUR SOLDIERS BEING EVACUATED FROM DUNKIRK UNDER HEAVY AIR ATTACK. SHIPS OF THE ROYAL NAVY STANDING BY. SMALL BOATS ASSISTING."

[*33*]

What could that mean—small boats assisting? How could small boats survive the kind of air attack the Germans laid down?

He read on. The King of Belgium *had* surrendered, leaving the British and French troops open to attack from the north. To avoid being cut off from Dunkirk—the only Channel port left—and to hold up the Germans to the south, the Allies had opened sluice gates near Gravelines. That flooded ground made Nazi tank attacks impossible. In a surrounded area of about twenty-five square miles, the B.E.F. and remnants of the French forces fought off annihilation and waited to be evacuated.

Mr. Lyons went to his office in a daze. His secretary at once handed him two messages, both marked "Urgent." One was to call his home at once. The other was from Bart Gordon.

The telephone line to Middle Pentworth was busy. Asking his secretary to call the other, Mr. Lyons reached Bart Gordon on the first try.

Bart's voice was lively. "Got last-minute reservations for Alan and Cicely on a ship sailing from Liverpool this Wednesday," he said. "Sorry it doesn't give you much time to get the kids ready. Sooner they get off, the better, the way things look

*The Allies had opened sluice gates
near Gravelines*

in France, don't you think? I've cabled my wife to meet them in New York. Okay with you folks?"

Mr. Lyons felt stunned when he hung up the phone. Then the call to his home came through, and he heard his wife's voice, shaken in a way he'd never heard it before.

"David!" she cried. "Thank heaven you're back. Alan has disappeared. He and Rod have been gone since Saturday, and we have no idea where they are. Nobody's seen them or heard from them."

CHAPTER FOUR

The Channel Shores

ON SATURDAY afternoon, after his father had left for Ireland, Alan hurried over to Rod Small's home. Earlier, he had arranged with the truckman, Alf Whitty, to give them a ride as far as the Lyons cottage on the shore of the Channel.

Rod, wearing a sweater with an Indian head knitted in the design across the chest, was shooting arrows at a tree. Archery was Rod's special sport, and he was very good at it.

Alan came right to the point. "Coming with me to the shore? We can go with Whitty in his lorry. How about it, Hiawatha?"

Rod threw down his bow and quiver and retorted, "Don't try to be funny."

"Will your parents let you go?" Alan asked.

"They aren't home," Rod replied. "They've gone to my aunt's. We'll probably be back before they are."

Alan nodded. "Right. We've got to hurry. C'mon."

When they raced into Whitty's garage, the trucker was tightening the cords of the tarpaulin over his load.

Ten minutes later the lorry was rolling briskly along the highway toward the coast, encountering frequent streams of military vehicles.

The air was soft and balmy, the countryside dappled with fruit trees in bloom and, along the brook running beside the road, wild flowers and bluebells. Except for stops to get permission to pass road barriers, the truck rattled along without interruption.

As they approached the shore Alan looked around curiously. "Crackey," he said, "everything around here's changed." In the large meadows, scattered piles of ancient farm machinery and old cars had been piled high to prevent enemy glider landings. At every main intersection stood army huts and knots of intrenched soldiers.

The boom of guns to the east, across the Channel, was familiar these days, but today the steady drum seemed heavier than Alan had ever heard.

"It sounds as though there's something strange happening down here," he said, after listening closely for several minutes. "Maybe we oughtn't to—"

"They're clobbering the Germans," Alf Whitty stated proudly. "That's our Nyvy ships making all that clump."

This satisfied the boys, who had been too busy

with their own plans to listen to the radio news-casts recently.

A few miles beyond Littlehampton, the boys climbed down at a small by-road branching off toward the sea. Whitty warned, "I'll be back in an hour, lads. Mind ye're 'ere waitin' when I come along. Don't want t'catch no cross words from yer folks fer keepin' ye out after dark."

Alan agreed. "I just have to get a few things from our cottage down this road. Take us ten minutes."

They trudged along the narrow lane. Alan stared ahead, more and more puzzled as they went on. "There *is* something funny going on," he said to Rod. "Look at those soldiers around our cottage. They don't belong there."

He broke into a lope and a few yards farther reached the end of the lane. Just beyond, some cottages faced the sea, separated from the inland downs by a fringe of small trees. The boys pushed through a hedge, slid down a small slope that ended behind one of the cottages, and pulled up short.

"Steady there, lads," said a grinning, armed soldier. "Where d'ye think you're going?"

"This is my house," Alan said in a startled voice. "Can't I go in?"

The soldier called over his shoulder to an older

sergeant. From the Channel came the constant chug of boat motors. And Alan noticed that the dozens of small pleasure craft that usually rode at anchor just off-shore were missing.

The grizzled non-com who answered the sentinel's call looked down sternly at the boys.

"This place is out-a-bounds, lads," he said gruffly. And to Alan, "Would you be young Lyons?"

At Alan's nod, he explained, "Defense Minstry's taken over your villa. Your belongings are over at Cap'n Peacock's—moved them yesterday. You'll find him down at his jetty—unless he's already left."

"Left for where?" Alan asked. *"What's going on around here?* Are *we* invading *Germany?"*

"Lumme," exclaimed the soldier, "I wisht we was. All those craft you see in the Channel are putting out to rescue the British Expeditionary Force from the beach at Dunkirk. Been at it three days now."

The information came so unexpectedly that both boys swung about to look at the sea, speechless.

They could see that all the sea traffic was eastward bound. At one small pier a navy truck was discharging cans of fuel, which were being handed down by sturdy, blue-clad men into a launch.

Alan pointed to it, and shouted, "There he is, Rod! That's the *Clara Belle,* and Captain Peacock's on deck. Let's hurry."

The truth was that both boys had momentarily forgotten the original reason for their errand to the seaside. They bore down on the jetty below the navy truck, and Alan shouted, "Captain Peacock, I must see you!"

The old seaman looked up for a moment from his work at the little boat's stern only long enough to bellow, "Alan Lyons! What're ye doing down here? You boys go back where ye came from as fast as ye can."

Alan remembered what he'd come for. Climbing down to the deck, he said hurriedly, "Captain, we're looking for some things from our cottage. I'm going to America. They told me up at the house that our goods were in your sail loft."

Without a pause to look up, the old man said, "Aye, they are. Get what ye want and push off for home fast."

But Alan, with Rod following him onto the deck, lingered.

"Are you going somewhere, Captain?" he asked rather foolishly since the answer was quite obvious.

Still without lifting his head, the seaman replied, "I am—as soon as I can get a hand to help. My mate—young Beckett—was called up for the army last week." A moment later he completed his chore, ran up the British flag at the stern, and jumped off the deck, herding the two boys before him.

"I'm off t' Dunkirk," he announced as they walked quickly along the narrow promenade above the wharfs. He gave both boys a brisk clap on the shoulder, pointed the way to his loft, and started off up the quayside toward a crowd of men working at the nearest warehouse.

[*43*]

Rod said, "C'mon, let's get your stuff and hustle back. Maybe we can do *something*." As this seemed sensible, they raced for the captain's loft, found the articles they'd come for, and were clambering down a ladder when cries, the scream of a warning klaxon, and the drone of approaching planes brought them to a tumbling halt. Picking himself up, Alan bolted through the door and spied the captain coming back from the warehouse with a younger, very burly sailor. Not two hundred feet up, a German dive bomber was making a sweep over the dockside, spitting machine-gun bullets. Behind it, but higher, came two British Spitfires.

Alan dived back inside the loft, pushing Rod into the fishy darkness. There came a bedlam of warning shouts, then a crash, the sudden burst of a fuel explosion, and the diminishing beat of plane engines.

Alan rushed out and stared down the roadway. Where Captain Peacock and the big sailor had been a minute earlier, a knot of workmen bent over a huddle of clothing on the pavement. Soldiers with a litter were rushing from the warehouse, and a military policeman was shouting orders. Dockside firemen were racing with their gear toward a building from which dense black smoke and flames were billowing. From its roof the bullet-riddled tail of the Junkers stuck up harmlessly.

The Spitfires were nearly out of sight.

Alan and Rod moved slowly forward, and were relieved to see that Captain Peacock had escaped and was hurrying toward his own boat. The two boys jumped onto the deck after him.

Alan asked, "What happened, sir?"

Captain Peacock glared at him. "Ye saw, didn't ye?" he snapped. "That ruddy Nazi plane 'e blasted us with 'is filthy bullets, and the man he struck down was the only chap outa the lot who'd agree to go to Dunkirk with me in the *Belle*." He hauled a watch out of his pocket, and glowering at it, growled, "I should've been on me way these three days ago."

He began to stare at Alan. A frown deepened his sharp gray brow, but his eyes were keen and thoughtful.

Perhaps, thought the boy, I wonder if— He burst out, "Take *me* with you, Captain! You know I can handle the *Clara Belle*—I've done it every summer. Please!"

The captain nodded, "Aye, you did," and continued to look at him calculatingly.

Rod also pushed forward.

[*45*]

"Take us both. I c'n help," he urged.

Peacock had made up his mind. "Alan, I'll sign ye on. You're a staunch lad. But you—Rod's yer name? There'll not be an inch of extra room when we start pickin' up the sojer lads. I'm sorry, but ye'd best be off home."

Rod protested, "But I don't take up much room, Captain."

The old man was adamant. "I don't know yer parents, son, and I got no license to risk taking ye," he stated flatly.

This was hardly the ending of the lark Alan or Rod would have expected.

"How about taking my bundle home, Rod?" Alan asked. "And you'd better hurry or you'll miss Whitty. Also, please go tell my mother where I've gone. She might be worried." Rod hesitated awkwardly, then suddenly making up his mind, he pulled off his sweater and tossed it to Alan. "You'd better take this sweater, anyway. It'll be cold on the water."

Standing on the dock, he found it hard to say good-by but managed to get out, "G-good luck," and watched wistfully as the boat's old engine throbbed into action.

The *Clara Belle's* low gunwale slid away from

the jetty, and the little craft heeled as she swung about and headed eastward into the Channel.

Slipping between the empty buoys, Captain Peacock settled down to the wheel. "Well, lad, the Royal Navy asked us to 'elp, and 'ere we come."

Alan laughed softly. "Captain Peacock, I notice you never drop your aitches unless you're excited."

The old sailor drew himself up. "Me excited?" he glowered, his blue eyes snapping. "The Nazi don't live could scare me."

Alan giggled, for the first and last time on that fateful errand of the *Clara Belle*.

CHAPTER FIVE

The Ordeal at Dunkirk

THE days that followed the beginning of the Dunkirk evacuation were a nightmare for the people of Britain. The government gave out bulletins of the rescue of British soldiers from France cautiously. The news was frightening and its meaning difficult to grasp.

Along the English coastline the inhabitants of the southern cliffs and downs that ringed the Channel were cheered by seeing streams of RAF planes cruising overhead. And by the sight of trains bearing battle-scarred, weary troops, just disembarked from some vessel that had managed to bring them safely home. But how many brothers and sons and fathers could be rescued from the German trap none knew.

Tuesday at Holmewood, Alan's father paced the

garden. He had returned home immediately after his wife had telephoned the news of Alan's disappearance. He could think of no way to find Alan that the police weren't better equipped to do. The boy had been away more than two whole days. How *could* Alan simply disappear?

Mr. Lyons was starting for the police station where he hoped some news might have come in when, from far down the street, Cicely's high-pitched cries halted him.

"Daddy, I've found him! *I've found him!*"

Racing down the street, leash flying, came a delighted Sireen with a flushed Cicely puffing behind.

Her father snorted in disappointment. He had thought Cicely meant her brother had returned. When the child finally caught her breath, she explained that the vicar had rescued Sireen from an abandoned shed. Suddenly Mr. Lyons noticed the forlorn figure of Rod Small coming wearily from the opposite direction.

He looked again. Rod was alone! When the boy reached the gate, Mr. Lyons asked anxiously, "Where's Alan?"

"That's what I came to tell you," panted Rod. "He's gone to Dunkirk."

"He's *what!*"

"He's gone to Dunkirk," Rod repeated. "That Captain Peacock had no one else to help him sail the *Clara Belle,* so he took Alan—*he* has all the luck. The captain said Alan knew how to handle the boat, but he sent me home because they needed all the space to carry soldiers."

Since Mr. Lyons seemed unable to speak, Rod went on, "Alf Whitty never waited for me with his truck, and I spent Sunday and part of Monday trying to sign on other boats going to Dunkirk. I had to walk all the way here, and I slept in a barn last night. I guess I better go tell my mother I'm back."

"Yes," Mr. Lyons said then, "you'd better."

The sound of the dog's barking had reached into the house, and as Rod plodded off toward home, Mrs. Lyons ran down the path. Disregarding Sireen's delighted greeting, she cried, "I thought Alan was here!"

When her husband had repeated Rod's story, she moaned, "That awful old man! How could he take Alan into *that!*"

"Now, my dear," Alan's father said, "Peacock won't take unnecessary chances with the boy."

But this was small comfort for either of them, because it wasn't really Peacock but the Germans whom they feared.

[*50*]

The day passed by without further news of Alan. Mr. Lyons had asked Sergeant Bottley to try to find out what had happened to the *Clara Belle,* but there was no word yet.

Bart Gordon had telephoned Holmewood several times, and suggested that although they might not be able to get Alan to Liverpool in time to sail for America, Cicely should go anyway. But neither Cicely nor her parents would agree to her going alone.

With his craft headed seaward Captain Peacock put her on course for the trip up the coast. He had been ordered to go first to a small naval station at Hastings for fuel and further orders.

"Now, boy," he said, "ye take the wheel while I go below and get the gear shipshape."

Alan steered watchfully, observing everything around him. He was now fully aware of the seriousness of the trip he had embarked on. It would be a long haul to Dunkirk, but he thought how lucky he was. The cool, salty wind made him feel vigorous and up to anything. Ships—old and modern—slipped past them. The long pier at Brighton looked dark and gloomy as the *Clara Belle* swept by in the twilight. Rounding Beachy Head, the waves slapped smartly against the vessel's bow, and a fine spray washed across the forward part of the cabin.

When darkness fell Captain Peacock took the wheel. All craft on the Channel that night were running without lights. The old sailor, his experienced mariner's eyes fixed intently on the depths of the darkness, his ears tuned to the sounds of the sea, had little to say. Alan stood beside him munching a sandwich, also alert.

The English coastline to their left was unlighted, somber, seemingly uninhabited. While still a long way from Hastings, Alan began to feel sleepy. A little ashamed of giving in so soon, he started below for a drink of water to wake himself up.

"Stretch out on the bunk, son, and get a few winks," the captain suggested. "I'll wake ye."

Alan had fallen asleep quickly and more deeply than he had intended, when he was thrown to the cabin floor by a tremendous jolt. Something slithered along the keel, there was a rending sound, and the engine screeched in crazy protest.

By the time he scrambled up on deck, the little launch was bobbing aimlessly in the swells.

Inspection showed no harm done to the hull,

but the propeller had been carried away by impact with floating debris.

"One of the hazards, dark like this," the old man grumbled. Then he settled back and said more cheerfully, "We'll have to wait for a tow, so we might as well rest. Go on with yer nap, and I'll keep an eye out for approachin' craft."

It seemed to Alan a poor start—losing a propeller. He could not go back to sleep but lay listening to the stillness and the faint throb of aircraft engines overhead. Presently, over these sounds he heard the beat of powerful marine engines drumming not far off. He climbed up to find Captain Peacock listening intently and trying to determine what the approaching craft was.

The churn of its wake became louder, then dimmed to a faint whisper.

"Why didn't you hail him?" Alan asked excitedly.

Unruffled, the captain replied, "Didn't know who he was. Might've been one o' those fast motorboats the Nazis send out at night. Sink us if they found us here."

Shortly afterwards, Alan heard the stranger's engines again over the slap of the waves. The boat was returning. Peering into the blackness, the two in the *Clara Belle* were suddenly bathed in a blinding circle of bright light. A voice from behind it shouted, "Ahoy, there. You in trouble, mate?"

Captain Peacock said quietly, "Must be one o' our chaps."

The RAF crash boat—which the stranger turned out to be—edged gently alongside, and Peacock said, "How did you know we were here?"

"We just picked a fighter pilot out of the water who had to parachute in not far from you," explained the N.C.O. in charge of the speedboat. "He saw you and tried to hit the briny alongside— he hoped you'd rescue him—but the wind carried him too far. We fished him out okay. So now, what's wrong here?"

When Peacock had explained their difficulty, the N.C.O. said, "Could be worse. I'll pass you a line and tow you as far as Hastings in a pig's wink, and you'll likely find a new propeller there. We must go on to our base near Folkestone."

He turned back to his own wheel and shoved off with the *Clara Belle* in tow wallowing along behind.

A little later a megaphoned voice from the darkened boat ahead called, "We're coming abreast of

Hastings now. Cast off when I give the word and head for the beach. I've signaled the Navy to come get you if you don't make shore." And after a few more minutes, another call: "Let 'er go—and good luck."

The *Clara Belle's* momentum took her grinding up onto the beach.

"Watch her now, son, until I get back," the captain ordered, and disappeared into the darkness to meet the beach patrol who came running to see what was up. Alan waited for the captain's return with two naval patrol men, and dozed a good part of the time.

By morning, with Navy assistance, the bent shaft was straightened and the new propeller was in place.

Some of the Navy repair crew had frowned at the *Clara Belle's* questionable seaworthiness and Alan's youthful looks, but the officer in charge had said, "Plenty of boats no bigger than you are going across, Captain. Pity to send out such small craft, but we need you."

The *Clara Belle* set off again and seemed not to know how tiny and foolish she was. Her engine pounding, she plodded along with many miles yet to cover.

Coming into the Dover Straits and the entrance to Folkestone Harbor, Alan stared. It was a sight which no one who had not seen it could have believed—so un-English it was, so weirdly unlikely. For steaming swiftly out or entering the harbor were flotillas of watercraft so incongruous, so battered and yet so staunchly businesslike that Alan exclaimed aloud.

"I'll take over now, son," Captain Peacock said. "Going to be a job getting through this traffic. Will ye look at that old tub!"

He pointed out a squat, badly scarred paddle-wheel steamer churning slowly and untidily toward the docks, her decks packed solidly with milling, cheering khaki-clad men. "I'll bet she's never been beyond the Thames mouth before in all her life."

"They'll have all the men back from Dunkirk before we get there," Alan shouted excitedly. "Hadn't we better hurry?"

"Just as soon as I get me orders," replied the captain.

The *Clara Belle* picked her way cautiously, waiting her chance to allow Captain Peacock to look for the control officer. Alan studied the crowded deck of an ancient light cruiser beside the dock. Along her rail, bandaged, bloody French and

British soldiers were stumbling, limp and weary, but good-naturedly urging each other on. Below them on the wharf, a line of officers, nurses, litter bearers, and ambulances waited. On the gangway some men hung back to lend a hand to buddies worse off than themselves.

Alan scowled. "They're all so cheerful."

"I suppose this ruddy 'arbor looks like 'eaven to 'em," the captain rumbled. "Why shouldn't they be 'appy? They're 'ome."

"There go his aitches again," Alan thought.

Peacock found the naval lieutenant who directed small boat traffic, and the *Clara Belle's* tanks were refilled at his order. The officer gave his instructions crisply. "You shouldn't have any trouble on the crossing to Dunkirk, skipper. Just follow the others. Nobody's going anywhere else. And you know the Channel tides are wicked—don't fool with them. When you get across, a beach-master—several are there directing fellows like you—he'll tell you what to do. Well, God speed."

The *Clara Belle* flounced about in an arc of spray and headed for Dunkirk.

"About five hours'll take us over, according to that Navy chap," Captain Peacock said a few minutes later. "How about a bite to eat?"

Alan teetered down the companionway and

came back with sandwiches wrapped in a napkin and a thermos jug of hot tea that a Red Cross man had handed aboard.

Three hours out from Folkestone, the sound of firing ahead grew noisier, and acrid, choking smoke began to taint the salty freshness of the wind.

Alan's nerves tightened, and he tugged at the chin strap of the helmet that had been given him by the Navy lieutenant. The old seaman glanced up now and then, listening for unseen Nazi bombers, but they could detect few planes. As the flat landscape around Dunkirk, blurred by smoke and haze, rose from the water Alan forgot everything except the stark grimness of the unfolding panorama. Moored offshore, several big British navy vessels trained their guns toward the menace of the sky. Between the larger ships and shore, small vessels were chugging out to the bigger craft.

Then, through the half-gloom, Alan caught sight of the beach and the long, snakelike lines of soldiers wading far out into the water. Other clusters of men moved up to take their places as, boatload by boatload, those at the head of the line were taken off.

Entering shallow water, the *Belle* was met by a small Navy picket boat whose skipper megaphoned, "Welcome, *Clara Belle*. Go on in. Pick up as many men as you can from those lines and take them out to yonder destroyer. Make use of this bombing lull. The Jerry planes'll be back— Best of luck!"

"Look, Captain." Alan pointed to the shore. "There are *thousands* of men over there. How can they wait there so patiently?"

But Captain Peacock had come to do a job, and he snapped, "No time for thinkin' now, lad."

Alan throttled the engine as they approached the line of men wading up to their chests in the swells, their faces black with grime. The captain leaned far over the side to grasp the arm of the first soldier. Heavy oil slicks from craft hit by shellfire shimmered on the surface and fouled both boats and waiting men. Spluttering, the man was dragged over the bulwark with a disgusted grunt. He spat out the dirty salt water he'd taken in a gasp, rolled back onto his feet, laughed, and immediately crouched to help with the next.

"Sorry t'muck up yer nice little boat, Commander," the soldier wheezed. While Alan jockeyed the launch to keep in position, man after man was hauled in, to the running cajolery and scolding of the others. "Now then, Halbert, 'ow

can we 'aul ye in if ye thrash abaht like a ruddy w'ale?" And when one man fell aboard, bringing a great wash of scum, "Wipe yer feet, lad. 'Ave a mind fer the decks!"

Cursing their own and each other's clumsiness,

more than thirty of the sodden men clambered over the side, till the *Clara Belle* lay dangerously low in the water. Only then did Captain Peacock shout, "That's all this trip." He signaled Alan to pull about hard while another small boat slid into their place. The *Clara Belle* set off cautiously through the choppy water to deliver her passengers to the destroyer.

Inshore, the sound of gunfire had been almost incessant. Artillery shells from encircling German positions sent up occasional towers of water, and the guns of the British ships standing by lobbed volleys of shells at unseen targets. The fog was lifting, and suddenly Alan heard aircraft engines overhead. He was barely conscious of the sound when a bomb struck, and a great column of water spouted just beyond the destroyer. It was followed by two more astern, sending up other thundering cascades. Then a fourth bomb hit the taffrail of the warship, glanced off into the sea, narrowly missing the overloaded *Belle* and again drenching the men in her. They sat crouched, grim and patient, prepared for anything.

Alan felt himself trembling from the shock, but he saw the men's patient stoicism and took heart.

The *Belle* lay among several small boats crowded together seeking to transfer their own loads to the destroyer. Captain Peacock was finding it difficult to bring her alongside the gangway that led up to the destroyer's deck. Just as Alan reached for a gangway stanchion, the warship took another hit on her stern. At the same moment, there was an underwater explosion and the *Belle* was pitched helplessly sideways in the violent upsurge. But, skilfully maneuvered away from collision with the big ship and the other small boats, she rode out the riotous crashing of the angry waters without losing a man. Many, however, had been washed into the vortex from boats which had capsized. Quickly regaining the gangway, Peacock swiftly discharged his own passengers, and went out to help pick up those still floundering in the swirling seas. Most of them came up grinning, and one said to Alan, "After a week or two you won't hardly notice them bombs no more."

A moment later, helping the captain and one of the stronger men ease from the water an unconscious seaman with a bad chest wound, he forgot everything except the need to get the half-drowned victims into the *Belle*.

"Better take that sailor out to the hospital ship, Skipper," one of the destroyer's officers shouted. "Our sick bay's stacked three deep already, and he needs a doctor in a hurry." Alan carefully tucked blankets around the drenched, wounded man, and the *Belle* headed a quarter of a mile out into the Channel where a white ship marked with red crosses rocked.

On the way, the seaman opened his eyes, stared up at Alan, and whispered hoarsely, "I got a kid at home no bigger'n you, sonny. At least, I *hope* he's home." Before Alan could think of a reply, Peacock said, "Now, shellback, here we are. The doctor'll fix you up as soon as we get you topside." A litter was lowered over the rail. The seaman was stowed safely in it and hauled gently up and as gently eased away for medical care.

This immediate mission accomplished, the little craft resumed her job.

From then on it became an almost steady shuttle from the lines on the beach to one of the larger vessels. Exhaustion settled down like a fog on the *Belle's* two-man crew, as on the scores of other crews moving patiently back and forth. Alan said, "We don't seem to be accomplishing anything. Every time we come back there're just as many men waiting as there were when we came."

The old man muttered, "Aye. Seems so."

The wearier Alan grew, the more he marveled at the jauntiness of the soldiers and at the daisies and poppies they had stuck in their helmets.

A limp little mutt was held tenderly on the shoulder of one soldier. When he handed the dog up to Alan, he begged, "Down't let 'im fall overboard, son." Settled down in the crowd on deck, he explained, "I couldn' leave 'im to the Nazis, could I? The trouble is, the poor little tike don't know wot I say. 'E only understands French."

Toward morning, the control officer called to Captain Peacock, "Pull down the beach a way and get some rest, sir, while you can."

The old mariner stiffened, but a glance at Alan made him nod. "Aye, aye, sir. Perhaps you're right." And so they lay for a time, riding quietly at anchor, beyond where the Channel surge was breaking. Alan curled up on blankets heaped beside the engine, and the old man stretched out, numb with fatigue, on the *Clara's* cabin bunk.

The launch rocked gently in the soft swells, and for a time Alan lay thinking drowsily of Cicely and home. They'd all be asleep, he supposed, and knew nothing more until a voice hailed him awake suddenly from the water below the deck.

"I say," the voice called softly but insistently, "how about giving me a lift out to one of those ships going home?"

Alan jumped up and looked down at the youth

in the water. At the sight of Alan, he tossed a large white bundle onto the deck.

"Who are you?" Alan demanded. It flashed through his mind that this might be a German spy.

The young man shook water from his face and laughed. "I might ask you that, too, if you weren't as English as Yorkshire pudding, lad. Help me aboard, will you? I've no mind to be captured by Jerries at this point. I'm RAF, kid. Got shot down yesterday by one of those ruddy Messerschmitts. Had to jump. Careful of my chute, will you? I've carried that baby for miles, and I don't want to lose it now."

Wet and shivering in the chill wind, he glanced curiously around and added, "You aren't doing this job alone, are you?"

Alan shook his head. He went to the cabin hatch and called down, "Captain Peacock. Will you come up, sir?"

But the heavy snoring of the old seaman was the only answer that came back, and the newcomer laughed. "Been at this filthy job a long time, eh?" At Alan's nod, he said, "Shame to wake up the skipper. But they need me back home at the squadron, and I've got to get across the Channel somehow. Do you think he'd put me on one of those transports out there? Right away?"

Alan made up his mind quickly. "I'll take you," he said. Noticing the pilot's teeth chattering, he pulled off Rod's sweater and handed it to him. "Here, you need this more than I do."

Between them they got the engine chugging and the anchor up. With Alan at the wheel, they headed out into the dark water. "My name's O'Neil—Dubbs O'Neil," the flier said presently. "What's yours?"

Alan told him and added that he had a brother flying Spitfires in the RAF. "That is, he's just gone to a fighter squadron, and maybe you know him?" he asked shyly.

"New lot of pilots came in just as I was leaving," the flier replied absently. "I say, there's a beggar just pushing off. I'll wager he's heading for Dover."

They had chugged up abreast of a low-lying large tug, crowded with soldiers. Alan shouted, "Ahoy, there, tug. Wait! Got room for one more?"

A voice from the rail replied, "Aye. Come alongside here."

For all Alan's care the two craft met with a jarring thump.

O'Neil had just leaped onto the tug's deck and Alan was pushing off, when Captain Peacock's voice rang up the steps. "What's that jolt, lad? Are we aground?"

For all Alan's care, the two craft met with a jarring thump.

"No, sir," Alan shouted back. "We had another passenger. One of our pilots."

The captain climbed on deck, yawned, and having wakened enough to see what had happened, said simply, "Good job, lad. I never heard a sound. And to think I got that tired working of a Sunday. First time I ever broke the Sabbath Day in me life."

By Monday noon the line of men waiting evacuation had begun to thin. With each hour the gunfire inland came closer to the sea, and the men who trailed down to the beach seemed nearer total exhaustion. German planes continued to appear, and one of their bombs fell on a paddle-wheel steamer into which the *Clara Belle* was loading. It carried away the *Belle's* mast. When Alan pulled himself out of the huddle of men who had ducked together, he found that a hot shell fragment had sliced under his helmet and gouged his chin. The steamer's medic hurriedly applied a bandage.

The grizzled old captain looked at Alan ruefully. "You're a casualty now, lad." He smiled grimly. "Your dad isn't going t'thank me for that."

Late that afternoon word spread that the Navy believed Operation Dynamo had about completed its mission, but among the little craft the end wasn't noticeable for many hours. " 'Tis the rear guard we've got to save from the Germans now, if we can," old Peacock declared belligerently. And, except for an hour's rest during darkness, they kept pace with the most persistent of the craft that, undamaged and still afloat, ran in and out through the din.

The final loading was the worst. The last of the stragglers who clawed their way aboard were almost unable to speak. One, who could, said that the Germans were closing in on the last few miles of free French soil along the Channel. Machine-guns were spitting fire over the beach, and Captain Peacock had to zigzag his way back to a cruiser that was to take off the last of his hollow-eyed cargo.

Resting on the engine hatch while the soldiers were being helped onto the navy ship, Alan saw that the old man was sitting as erect as ever, but that his head drooped unconsciously, and every so often his eyes closed. Alan could no longer think clearly himself, but he roused when a naval officer ran down the gangway and shook the old man's shoulder.

"You've had enough, Skipper," the lieutenant said. "And done a wonderful job. No need to tell you the Navy knows it. We'll give you a tow back to Dover."

*Operation Dynamo had about completed
its mission*

Captain Peacock tried to rise, but the officer stopped him. "No arguing now. Just stand by to take our line, and God willing, you'll be in Dover within a few hours."

Dimly, Alan was aware of orders barked from the battleship's decks overhead, and the jerk as the *Belle* responded to the tow. The white cliffs of Dover, he thought, I'm going to see them soon . . .

But the next thing he was conscious of was the timbers of a jetty where the *Clara Belle* lay rocking gently.

CHAPTER SIX

England Awaits the Invasion

A POLICE car skimmed through the countryside of southern England on Wednesday. Seated between a Brighton constable and Sergeant Bottley, Alan said stiffly, "You needn't have come for me. We brought the *Clara Belle* back to the captain's moorings this morning, and I'd have found some way to get home."

Sergeant Bottley glanced at the tired, grubby boy beside him and asked sharply, "Did ye know yer folks 'ave been fair raging with worry over you?"

Alan looked startled. "But I sent word by Rod Small where I was going," he explained.

"Aye," Bottley said. "But 'e didn't get 'ome till late yesterday."

Alan, still hazy about time, after his days under fire, asked curiously, "How did you know that Captain Peacock and I were back?"

"Ah, that," Bottley said smugly. "Well, the Nyvy kept track of you—informed our station this morning, early."

Alan subsided drowsily until the car reached Middle Pentworth. At the gate to Holmewood, however, he leaped to the curb and shouted, "Sireen's back!" The dog had begun to yelp and claw at the gate.

Mrs. Plume opened the door, gave one startled look, and bellowed, "Missus Lyons! Alan's 'ome!"

Between Sireen's violent welcome and Mrs. Plume's embrace, Alan was barely able to edge himself up the brick walk to the door. Halfway there, Cicely started to throw her arms around him, but hastily recovered with a frowning "My word! You *are* filthy." Then his father and mother came out, crying, "Oh, Alan, you're home safe!"

And Cicely shrieked, "We've lost our chance to go to America! The ship sailed this morning."

A few answers to his parents' questions got him as far as the living room. Here Mrs. Plume, who had held her tongue thus far, refused to ignore the state of his clothes any longer.

"If yer'll jest run upstairs now, duckie," she

said, "and tyke off them rags, and run a nice 'ot bath, ye'll feel a lot better." Whereupon she veered toward the kitchen to concoct a suitable feast for her prodigal.

His mother had immediately begun to fuss about the dirty bandage on Alan's chin. But his father, concealing his great pride fairly well, said calmly, "Just a scratch, I expect. He's safely home now."

Once scrubbed and fed, Alan sat down to talk over the last few days with his father, and suddenly remembered the bundle he had turned over to Rod.

"Not that I need it now," he said, "but that's really what we went down to the seaside for. I honestly didn't know about Dunkirk when we started, Dad."

His father replied, "I knew things in France were coming to a peak, but I didn't realize how soon, either, till I got back from Dublin." He added, "You lost your chance to go to America, you know."

"I wish Rod could have gone in my place," was all Alan could think of to reply.

Then, remembering the report a naval commander had made to the *Clara Belle's* crew, he said,

"We helped bring home over three hundred thousand of our own troops and a lot of Frenchmen. But most all their equipment had to be left to the Jerries."

"That's a heavy loss," Alan's father sighed. "But it's a miracle that so many men were saved. We shouldn't complain."

Bart Gordon, making the rounds of plane factories and airdromes, found few opportunities to visit Holmewood in the next few weeks.

Meanwhile a round-roofed, corrugated metal air-raid shelter was sunk into the family garden, to Mrs. Lyon's dismay, where some of the choicest flower beds had been.

"Makes me feel as if we were going to earth like hunted foxes," she said crossly as she stowed tinned food on its shelves. Elsewhere in England the same ugly, arched shelters, issued in great numbers by the government, were crowded into tiny backyards or beautiful lawns.

Bart Gordon finally showed up one Saturday. At the station he greeted Alan with, "You're a fine one, my lad, to go traipsing off after I wangled space on a boat for you two kids. Don't you want to go to America?"

In his mind, Alan had been preparing for this

question. "Well, I do appreciate all you've done, sir," he replied slowly. "But now I'm not awfully sure I want to go."

Bart studied him for a moment. "I can understand that, though I don't agree with you. You shouldn't stretch your luck too far. Oh, by the way—" He stuck a fist in his pocket and pulled something out. "Here's a little gimmick I think I should give you to keep. That's my own good luck token. You need it, by the looks of things."

Alan took the heavy silver piece in his hand. "Thanks, sir," he said. "Is it an American coin?" He examined it closely.

"Yep. It's a U. S. silver dollar. One buck."

Late May and early June was a bad period for the people of Britain. Though the shock of Dunkirk wore off, they had to learn to endure one wartime disaster after another. Five days after the great epic of the Dunkirk evacuation, Norway surrendered to the powerful German Army following a long, gallant effort to save herself. Four days after that, Paris was in the hands of the Germans, and on June 25, France gave up the war.

The inhabitants of Middle Pentworth went about their business tight-lipped, especially when Prime Minister Churchill declared: "We shall fight

They had to learn to endure one wartime disaster after another

on the beaches . . . in the fields and in the streets. . . ."

The government issued an order that no church bells were to be rung henceforth except to warn that a seaborne invasion of the British Isles had begun. Older men in still larger numbers began to drill for Home Guard duty in every village, sometimes using broomsticks when they had no guns. And after a week's leave, the rescued troops from Dunkirk went back to training with their regiments.

Mr. Lyons occasionally had lunch with Bart Gordon, who looked on the war situation as puzzling and ominous.

"I can't for the life of me figure out why Hitler hasn't followed up his victories in France with worse attacks on England," Bart said. "He's got the troops and tanks and planes. But all he's doing is staging a raid here and there around your Channel ports and airfields."

"We aren't complaining," muttered David Lyons drily. Then he added more soberly, "What the Germans are planning is perfectly obvious. If they're going to knock out England they must move with everything in top form. Since Goering has to have airfields close to British targets, I think they're probably building up those airdromes they took from France and the Low Countries. They all must have been badly battered by the time the French collapsed."

"I've heard," Bart said, "that the old-line German officers detest Hitler, especially the way he interferes because he believes he has some kind of divine military guidance."

"To me," Lyons said, "Rudolf Hess is the mystery man of that Nazi troop. He's a flier, and a close friend of Hitler's. But I don't see just what his role is."

"He's the weirdest character in that whole Nazi bunch," Bart agreed. "I don't suppose we'll ever know what such a man'll do next."

Bart Gordon's remarks about the trouble between the German General Staff and Hitler were quite true. The German leader had signed a peace pact with Russia to give him time to complete Britain's conquest without interference from Russia. But Hitler still believed that England might be tamed without a fight.

"Why," he stormed, "should an Anglo-Saxon country like Britain fight other Anglo-Saxons like us? They'll see things our way if we give them a good scare."

While his staff proceeded with plans for staging

Operation Sea Lion—a cross-Channel sea-land assault on the British Isles—he fiddled and interfered, and the summer slipped by.

Since the Luftwaffe had proved to be his most decisive weapon so far, the Fuehrer told Goering to go ahead with the terror bombings that were to soften up Britain. And so, on August 5th, after the Anglo-Saxon British failed to show the slightest sign of joining forces with his own, he gave the fateful go-ahead. After a long period of bad weather, terrible sky-borne warfare started that was to be called The Battle of Britain.

Alf Whitty, the truckman who had taken Alan and Rod to the seashore, continued to make his rounds all that summer.

During the first week in August Alan was on his way home after doing an errand for his mother. He had gotten off the bus on the outskirts of Middle Pentworth when he saw Whitty's lorry chugging in from the country and Alf, dead white, sitting as though he were in a trance in the cab. Alan ran out into the road, stopped him, and clambered up.

"What's the matter?" he demanded.

Alf pointed to a burned triangle of fabric dangling from the roof of the lorry.

"Got meself into something, this trip," he groaned. "The Jerries come over to give that big airdrome at Shoreham a terrific pasting, an' I 'ad ter jump and leave me lorry on the road. See, a bomb tore the roof. It's getting so that shore ain't a safe place fer nobody."

But he brightened a minute later and added, "I seen five or six o' them Nazi planes go down, any-how."

Suddenly they heard the sound of fire engines, and noticed columns of smoke rising from two points on the opposite side of the village.

"Speed up, Alf," Alan begged. "Something's happened here, too."

Catching up with one of the town's raid ward-ens, Alan called, "What's happened?"

The man replied, "A Jerry plane ditched its bombs over yonder and hit a couple of houses."

"Blinking Jerries," muttered Alf angrily. Be-fore they had reached the scene they met another warden coming away from it, and stopped for news. "No use going on there," the man said. "A little villa and the ice-house knocked to splinters, but nobody got 'urt."

At his own corner Alan thanked Whitty and said, "I'll get out here. You'd better get home yourself, Alf."

When Alan rounded the gate into his own yard,

Cicely came bounding out and shouted gleefully, "What do you think, Alan? That bomb hit the Plumes' house, and they're coming to live with us. Isn't that wonderful? Plumey and Ole Dickie, too!"

All Alan could think of at the moment was "Gor!" Mrs. Plume's husband, "Ole Dickie," was the favorite of no one but his devoted wife.

But there were other things to think about. The main British airdromes along the coast were now being subjected to thorough, back-breaking attacks by the Luftwaffe—intended to cripple the RAF. And when the German pilots were driven away from these targets by British fighters and anti-aircraft fire, bombs were often dumped on defenseless homes and people—as had happened to the Plumes.

The air of tension increased. One of the more disturbing pieces of gossip was Bart Gordon's report that the RAF was losing a dangerous number of planes and pilots in their outnumbered duels with the continuing German assaults. And now Peter was flying as a full-out fighter pilot!

One day when Bart was at Holmewood, there was a telephone call from Peter himself. When the family had had their chats with him, Bart took the phone, and to his comments, Peter replied, "Right. Flying against the Luftwaffe is rugged, but you'd be surprised how quickly you get used to it. It's the poor blighters who have to stay in the ground control stations that I'm sorry for. They can't get away. You know, the Jerries have stopped pounding airdromes, and have begun to strike

hard at wireless installations. You ought to see the damage they've done to some of our sector stations. It isn't just the chaps in the radio-telephone rooms that have to stand it. It's the WAAF operators, too. Some gals!"

A telephone operator's voice cut in. "Sir," she said sternly, "I'll have to cut you off. Giving mili-

tary information to civilians is forbidden." And to Bart Gordon's chagrin the line went dead.

"I'm sorry, Dave," he said. "I was a fool to let Peter spout off like that."

Mr. Lyons laughed. "Don't worry about Peter. He wouldn't give away any secret stuff."

As a single bright spot, an air raid on Berlin, carried out at Churchill's order about this time, gave great satisfaction to many Britishers.

Having the Plumes living in the house held both advantages and disadvantages. "Ole Dickie," who had been given a couple of medals for his services in World War I, suffered from the after-effects of poison gas in his last engagement. Though a bulky, once-muscular man, he was no longer up to much beyond recounting his wartime experiences and doing a few simple chores.

The fact that Bart Gordon had been unable all summer to obtain passage again for the children to go to America, didn't stop the old veteran's talking as though they expected to leave at any moment. One of his chores was polishing the family's shoes, and he grumbled about the state Alan's boots were in. One night in September, he ambled into the living room where Mr. Lyons was studying the evening paper and held out a pair of disreputable-looking shoes.

"Will 'ee look at these boots, sir!" he demanded. " 'Tis a shame a respectable lad must go orf t'America in such shabby gear. And 'tain't for lack o' polishin'."

Alan's father did look, and exclaimed, "Oh, I say, they are done for, aren't they? And now that I think of it, his mother's been saying he should go up to London for a new pair."

CHAPTER SEVEN

Alan Sees the London Docks

IT WAS decided that Alan was to go to London with his father in a day or two. Accordingly, on the Saturday morning of September 7, he scrambled aboard the train with the promise of a whole day to see the sights.

Going immediately to the boot shop when they reached town, his father saw him properly fitted and then took him to the club where they were to have lunch with Bart Gordon.

At lunch in the club, Bart said, "Dave, I have to run down to the docks to check on a shipment of engines. How about Alan going along?"

Alan was delighted. "The docks? Oh, good! Please, Dad."

ALAN SEES THE LONDON DOCKS

His father agreed, and leaving the new shoes at the club, Bart and Alan went off together with a promise to be back at four-thirty.

They arrived by taxi to within a short stroll of the Tower Bridge where the London docks began. They stopped to buy apples from a pushcart. Children by the dozen were racing and screaming around barrows and carts and jutting house corners.

Alan and the American, with their gas masks slung over their shoulders, pushed through the crowds. They came to a slit between the rows of buildings where they caught sight of the superstructures of tall ships, and a maze of quayside derricks.

"We may have some trouble finding the old freighter I'm looking for, Alan," Bart Gordon explained. "Keep an eye out for the *Colfax Castle*. Army'll probably have a guard around her because she's packed with munitions besides those engines I'm after."

They skirted several bustling piers and great rusty steamers. The sound of donkey engines, the hoarse calls of officers and stevedores, and the creaking of block and tackle made a steady clatter, pierced by the shrill cries of circling sea gulls. They came to a fenced-off dock where two military

"That's our ship," Bart said

guards were posted at the wide gate, and gazed up at the name *Colfax Castle* lettered across a towering, salt-stained bow.

"*That's* our ship," Bart said. "Come along." But when he showed his pass to the guards, one of them said, "If you have no pass for him, we can't let the boy through the barrier." At Bart Gordon's frown, he added heartily, "Oh, we'll look after him, Yank, till you finish your business."

Alan felt crushed. He wanted particularly to go on board, but the guard repeated, "Orders are orders, sir. *Nobody* enters without credentials." After a moment Bart promised to be back within half an hour and ran up the gangway.

Alan found plenty of fascinating things to watch along the piers—cranes swinging massive crates over the ship's side, lorries loading, messengers on motor bikes coming and going, men checking cargo, naval officers shouting orders from the decks. But whenever he edged away from the gate he was abruptly summoned back by the red-faced, elderly guard.

Three quarters of an hour passed, and Bart Gordon hadn't reappeared.

Alan was wondering how far he dared wander away when, above the clatter of the dockside, a new sound rose—the wail of a siren. It was quickly joined by others until within moments the alarm seemed to engulf the whole riverside.

At the first rising note, Alan, hoping to catch sight of Bart, turned toward the ship's gangway.

At first there was a feeling in the air of arrested movement. Then, suddenly, the men poised on the gangway began to hurry down. The gates swung open, and they began a swift mass movement toward the road while, all up and down the riverside, ships' whistles blasted the "abandon ship" alarm.

Standing near the now-packed dock entrance, Alan heard a chief petty officer bark to another, "We've got seven minutes from the time the Jerries started across the Channel, to clear our area. Order your people away from this munition ship and get a move on to shelters."

Alan looked up at the sky anxiously, but could not detect the sound of planes. However, he heard, or felt, the clump of distant explosions, too far down the river to tell where they were. There was a milling of people all around him, and with a determined wave of the hand, his police guardian shouted to him over the heads of the crowd, "Run to the shelter with the others, sonny. Schoolhouse at the bottom of that street—where the crowd's heading."

But Alan, unwilling to leave without Bart, hung back, trying to keep on his feet in the mob. Above the sirens' wail, the military guard shouted in a sharper tone, "Get going, lad. I'll tell your friend where you are when he comes out." Now there came the faint drone of planes, and the guard's voice rose shrilly. "Blast it! Get going, boy!"

With the deep grumbling beat of the planes growing louder, helmeted raid wardens with arm bands impatiently waved onward people who came pouring from the houses, hurrying them toward the shelter spots. The towering volume of wailing sound seemed to freeze Alan's mind, and he slowed and turned back, hoping to catch sight of Bart.

From lower down the river the thundering beat of approaching aircraft grew loud, and a series of near explosions detonated with a dull roar. A heavy fire truck clanged down the road, and the moan of an ambulance struggling to get through meant that disaster had begun to take its toll.

When Alan stopped to stare up at the thick swarm of dark planes coming overhead, he saw with a horrid fascination sticks of bombs loop out from their bellies, and he crouched as they struck nearby roofs and burst. Both the dinning throb of the engines and the explosions seemed all around him.

He flung himself into the shelter of a doorway and, as a bomb buried itself among some warehouses, he shrank lower, watching in wonder the swift fury with which flames and acrid smoke spread everywhere. Flaming embers showered the road. Fire pumpers arrived, and on the river men were cutting adrift timber barges that were ablaze, to save the other ships. An incendiary bomb struck close to the *Colfax Castle*.

The sky glowed red, and choking smoke filled the narrow streets. Alan moved on, elbow to elbow with the rest of the people. Bart Gordon, he thought, would surely be ordered to go to the school too. The people around him were friendly, as though they all knew each other, which most of them did, and he found himself doing little things to help one and then another.

He had just aided a wispy and very talkative old granny over a mound of rubble, when a shout: "Get down!" was drowned by the thunder of a fresh flight of planes. People scattered to cellarways as a bomb hit the road, scattering paving stones and the remains of a pushcart filled with apples. A moment before, a large, blowsy woman had hauled the

cart up to the curb. Thinking fast, Alan pulled the
old granny down in a doorway and tipped a dis-
lodged shop sign over them both. Out of the corner
of his eye, he noticed the apple woman swing to
shield two small children in a doorway. The shock
of the explosion, the rain of rubble, and the crash
of falling window glass, paralyzed the street for a
moment, although the older woman never stopped
mumbling. Alan asked, "Are you hurt?"

The little old lady backed out from under the
signboard. "Not me," she complained crossly. "But
where's Maggie? That was 'er cart blowed up."

The apple woman needed nobody's help. She
was on her feet before the last of the debris fell,
calling, "You orl right, Aunt Bessie?" and tenderly
mopping at a bruise on the cheek of one of the children she had protected. "Stop yer bawlin' now,
duckie," she crooned hoarsely. " 'Ow about a nice
apple?

"Look there, sonny," she called to Alan, " 'and
us one, that's a good lad." Alan picked an undamaged apple out of the litter and presented it to the
child.

A sturdy-looking warden came loping over rubble to ask whether there were any serious casualties.
At sight of Maggie he pulled up short.

"Oh, *you're* here, Maggie," he grinned.

"I am," stated the big woman with ominous severity. Jerking a large thumb in succession at her shattered pushcart, Aunt Bessie, and the two children, she said, "Tom Gibbons, see wot them Jerries done with their ruddy bombs! Smashed me cart, an' like ter smashed the rest of us. Git these pore kids ter shelter, an' Aunt Bessie, too." She nodded toward Alan. "I don't know 'oo this lad is, but 'e's a bitta orl right. Took care o' 'isself and Aunt Bessie just now."

To the old lady, Maggie said, "You go along with Mr. Gibbons and the kids, like a nice girl, and they'll give yer some tea t'settle yer nerves."

The warden nodded patiently. "You're coming to the Keeton school shelter?" he asked. At Maggie's nod, he said, "Well, then stop off and see if you can pry those silly Trinkle sisters out of their lodgings in Roundkettle Lane and get them to shelter, will you? I've sent police to warn them and been in myself, but nobody can make them budge."

"Cor, the silly waifs," sighed Maggie. "I'll shoo 'em out. The lad, 'ere, and I'll be along in a jiffy."

Seeing Maggie in control of the street, the warden took the children's hands and asked the old woman if she could walk to the shelter. When

"Stop yer bawlin' now, duckie,"
she crooned hoarsely

she replied curtly that she "hadn't noticed that 'er legs was missing," he nodded and set off.

This was during one of the strange lulls between one black trail of planes and the next. But the familiar drone was growing near again and almost drowned out Maggie's shout to Gibbons: "Don't forget t'tell the commissioner I want ten guineas damage f'r me cart."

"Fat chance," Gibbons shouted back. "Three pounds, more like." He picked up the smaller child and started to run.

"Blimey," grunted Maggie, " 'ere come them ruddy bommers again. Can ye run, lad?"

With Maggie leading most of the way, they raced toward the corner of Roundkettle Lane. But before they could reach it, the familiar detonations behind them began, with the sound of falling timbers and the strange whistle and sizzle of flame, and they ducked into a cellarway.

Maggie looked down at Alan thoughtfully. "You seem a well brought up lad, ducks," she said. "But I don't remember seeing you around 'ere before." When Alan explained that he was visiting the dockside and had lost the friend he had come with, she said cheerfully, "Wot a shyme! But 'e's sure to 'ave gone t' the shelter. We'll find 'im."

[*98*]

The last of this well-meant speech was half lost in the roar of the planes and the rattle of buildings. But, propped against the ancient walls with her, Alan felt oddly reassured.

Maggie had a habit of darting, and the thunder of destruction had barely ended when she scrambled up the cellarway steps, and was off.

"The ruddy swine 'ave 'it Roundkettle Lane," she roared hoarsely. Against the horizon, fire raged with new violence, and smoke and dust thickened the air anew. Alan ran, following Maggie up and down piles of broken brick and timbers to one of the houses whose upper stories had collapsed into the roadway.

A lorry had already drawn up, and men were running in with picks, shovels, and other rescue gear. Maggie snatched a shovel and handed it to Alan. Going down on her knees beside the basement window, she told him, "Dig them bricks away." Then, tossing aside splintered bits of furniture, she smashed the glass and called through the space, "Aggie Trinkle! Minnie! MINERVA! Are you there?"

"We'll have to get inside," said a warden, and sank his pick into the rubble against the areaway door.

Alan worked till the sweat ran down his back and into his eyes, and yet he dreaded what he should see when they got the door opened.

Maggie pushed and hauled, pointed out where

to thrust shovels, muttering, "That's clever now—
over 'ere a bit."

When the door was free she scraped it wide open.
Kicking aside plaster and lath, she made her way

into the shambles.

A moment later she was back, pushing before
her a thin gnome of a woman with a teacup in her

hand. Behind crept an almost exact duplicate of her.

"We were just having ourselves a nice cuppa hot tea," the first woman stated crossly. "It was our best Oolong, too," explained the other.

"Well now, it's a pity you didn't go off to the shelter," the warden told them pointedly. "I've no doubt they'll fill your cups for you again at the school."

Maggie said not a word to them. Motioning to the warden to get the women away to safety, she said gruffly to Alan, "I won't feel right till we've made sure everyone wot lived in this block is out. D'yer think yer can dig a bit longer?"

Digging a bit longer turned into considerable hard work in the tumble of blocked passages and fallen walls. Maggie and a doctor applied splints and antiseptics and bandages, and ambulance workers came and went with their stretchers. Alan grew hotter and dirtier and so tired that he scarcely remembered ever doing anything else but dig. Everyone there was bone tired by that time. The smell of the cordite, of burning spice and sugar warehouses on the river, and the smoke had begun to dope their senses.

Maggie's hair stood on end, frosted with lime

and dirt. Her clothes drooped around her like the garb of a wind-tossed scarecrow. It was nearly seven o'clock by the warden's watch when she straightened up and said, "My! They *will* be wonderin' wot's keeping me, down at the shelter," and scrambled down off a heap of rubble.

"Bad mess, that," she offered absent-mindedly as they trotted up the darkening street.

CHAPTER EIGHT

The Beginning of the Blitz

Bart Gordon was deep in the hold of the *Colfax Castle* when the first sirens wailed. A warning horn rasped through the ship, and over the loudspeakers came the command: "Everybody off the ship—repeat—everybody off."

Bart and the Air Force officer, with whom he was checking, scrambled up ladders to the deck and joined the crush of shipworkers hurrying to leave. Bart looked wildly toward the entrance gate where air raid wardens were directing the way to shelters, but Alan was nowhere in sight.

Already the drumming sound of an enormous flight of planes shook the area. Bart turned to the officer at his side. "Not much warning time," he exclaimed. "The Jerries are almost overhead. *Where* is that boy?"

He pushed his way to one of the guards at the gate being buffeted by the swarming crowd.

"What about the lad I left in your charge?" he demanded.

The man pointed toward a street leading away from the docks. "I sent him to the school shelter just beyond. I couldn't let 'im wait for you, sir."

Bart was swept along, across the wide quayside where other wardens were herding the crowds. Thinking that Alan must have gone ahead, he had started to run when the drone of hundreds of planes became a roar.

He thought angrily: How *could* I have brought the boy down here? As the noise of the attack thudded and crumped, and flames began to flare up around him, he ran from one protected spot to another, expecting every moment to see Alan among the others hurrying to escape. Rescue workers, arriving by vehicle while the bombs still fell, set up new confusion. As one used to tackling physical problems, Bart Gordon set to lifting timbers and easing trucks over obstructions. Then, pressing on, he dashed from one safe spot to another, and after a little more than an hour he found the shelter he had been directed to.

David Lyons finished his deferred week-end work at the office by mid-afternoon. With ample time to meet Alan and Bart, he strolled through the busy streets toward his club. Sometime before he turned into the entrance, the lament of the first siren echoed across the sprawling city.

Although, before he had gone far, Mr. Lyons felt the tremor and heard the dull throb of distant aircraft, he was not greatly disturbed. During the past few months there had been numerous alarms in the city when small attacks were going on in other areas. He discovered that Bart and Alan had not returned to the club, and left word with the aged doorman to have them join him upstairs when they returned. Along with several members who were behaving rather excitedly, he went up to the club library where tea was being served. There he found an agitated group crowded around the tall windows facing east, staring at the sky. When David Lyons joined them he was astounded to see a huge, almost solid mass of dark German bombers with fighter craft above and below them spanning the horizon over the entire length of London's East End.

Thoroughly horrified, Mr. Lyons watched the flash of the first string of bombs exploding in the distance, followed by hundreds of incendiaries laying a lurid carpet of fires along the dockside.

Good heavens, he thought, Alan and Bart may still be down there.

He stood stiff with fear for them for a few moments, undecided what he ought to and could do. Then, unable to bear the suspense any longer, he raced down to hail a passing taxi, and directed the reluctant driver to take him to the Tower Bridge.

Persuaded by the promise of a whopping tip, the driver agreed. He managed to avoid the signals of bobbies, who had orders to keep traffic away from the dockside, and worked his way through at Mr. Lyons' direction.

At one point the taxi found its way completely blocked by snakelike fire hoses and a red bus upended against a building.

Mr. Lyons urged his driver to turn back and try another route, but the grizzled old fellow furiously slammed down the meter flag and refused to go on. There was nothing to do but continue on foot. Paying his fare and a bonus, Alan's father picked his way past the smoking rubble in the direction of the river and finally reached the docks.

He asked a bobby where the *Colfax Castle*, the ship Bart had said he was to visit, was berthed. The policeman replied, "Well, sir, she *was* down there beside the third pier. But she was blown sky high by a bad hit a few minutes ago."

"What about those on board?" Mr. Lyons asked.

The policeman shook his head vigorously. "The

watch got them all off as soon as the warning whistle went. Everyone was sent to that shelter where the signs lead to."

Mr. Lyons moved on. During the next half hour, bobbies sent him on detours of several blocks

around obstructions—one a large delayed-action bomb buried in the pavement, which was being cautiously examined by a demolition officer, one of the Army's "Death and Glory" boys. Many times David Lyons took refuge wherever he could, while fresh clouds of Luftwaffe craft throbbed in overhead, and the air shook under their crashing barrage. Eventually he traced his way back to the road he believed Alan and Bart must have been on, and found the school building he had been directed to.

He climbed the flight of sandbagged stone steps to the big doors and went in.

Inside, a welter of men, women, and children with their jumble of nondescript possessions crowded the classrooms. Nurses and first-aid workers moved among the frantic mothers and fathers looking for missing ones.

As Mr. Lyons passed through, he heard one warden complain to another, "You can't do nothin' with these people. They're too dazed to know what's good for 'em. Maggie oughter be here." Finding neither Alan nor Bart anywhere upstairs, Mr. Lyons went on to the basement where doctors and volunteer nurses were giving temporary care to the seriously wounded.

Somewhat to his relief, neither Bart nor Alan

was among these people either. He returned to the entrance and was crossing the crowded front hallway when a woman so big, so bedraggled, and yet so commanding that he involuntarily stopped to stare at her, swooped through the throng by the door. She gave the place a swift, sweeping glance, and at once little cries went up: "Maggie!"

She banged a cloud of dust from her tattered clothes, pushed her sleeves above her elbows, and shouted in a hoarse, jolly voice, "So 'ere's where yer all are, ducks. Well, they sye a spot o' schooling don't 'urt nobody." And her gusty laugh rolled out, bringing titters through the room.

The warden in charge strode up to her and said, "Maggie, we've orders to transfer this crowd out to the country, and some of 'em say they won't go."

She laughed. "Lumme, out there with all them trees and birds! Who blames 'em?" But she grinned, slapped his shoulder, and added, "Don't worry. We'll send 'em orf soon as yer omnibuses arrive."

Then, suddenly spotting those she was looking for, she turned and shouted at the top of her lungs, "The Trinkle girls got 'ere orl right, Alan!"

At this, David Lyons, who had been watching her in a tired trance, started. And the ragged, dust-laden lad who had been rinsing his hands in a bucket beside the door looked up over his shoulder to reply to Maggie, saw his father, and shouted, "Well, look who's here! Dad!"

Alan then had to explain to Maggie that David Lyons was *not* his lost friend Bart Gordon, but his father. When she understood the situation, Maggie frowned at the warden.

"*Think*, Tom Gibbons," she ordered him. " 'Aven't *yer* seen an American toff round 'ere anywheres?"

The warden looked surprised, and asked, "Thickish chap with one of them cowboy hats they wear in the cinema?"

"That sounds like our American friend," Alan laughed, and his father exclaimed, "Then you *have* seen him."

Gibbons exclaimed, "I orter. He's been in and out of this shelter a dozen times asking for the boy."

"Where's the man got to now?" Maggie snapped. "That's wot we want t'know."

Gibbons said, "I haven't the foggiest idea." But Aggie Trimble, who had been listening to them, piped up happily, "He's in the tellyphone boof."

And, at that instant, the door to a cubbyhole some distance down the hall banged open, and

[*112*]

Bart stepped out. He saw the group by the door and let out a full-throated, open-prairie "Great Jumping Jehoshaphat! Alan! Dave!"

Shouts and noises had begun outside, and a bobby came in to say that the first buses were arriving for the transfer.

"Aggie Trinkle!" Maggie scolded. "You knowed this boy was with me orl the time, and you didn't tell 'is friend. You and Minnie git along out into that bus afore I . . ."

As they scurried away, she said, "Don't mind Aggie. Them old girls ain't 'ad much fun in their lives. They love orl this excitement. It's better'n a cinema."

The crowd was being shepherded outside, but Tom Gibbons lingered to say to Alan, "We're beholden to you, lad, for all you've done with Maggie, though you'd no call to do it."

Mr. Lyons and Bart Gordon were getting nervous over the delay in leaving. Bart had found that the school phone wasn't working, and Mr. Lyons, anxious to reassure Alan's mother of their safety, wanted to get home as quickly as possible.

Alan's good-by to Maggie was as offhand as though they had spent the afternoon at a football match, and she said, "Come back an' see us some-

[*113*]

time, duckie, when we can 'ave a nice quiet chin."

Out in the street, Alan's father said, "No telling whether those bombers'll be back."

"Why shouldn't they?" Bart swept an arm across the flaming sky along the waterfront. "They won't need radar guides or maps tonight to find the target with those fires lighting the way."

Plodding carefuly among the obstructions, the three trailed away through the ruddy gloom of London.

Before they reached the club, the new night raids began. Fresh salvos of fire bombs plummeted through the searchlight shafts and shrapnel bursts into the glowing embers where old fires were barely under control, and set them blazing fiercely again.

From the windows of the club Alan looked out and saw the eerie orange light glinting on the bombers' wings.

"It wasn't like this at Dunkirk," he told Bart, who was watching beside him. "Over there you felt it was soldiers fighting soldiers on the beach. But this afternoon the Jerries attacked all those poor people who couldn't help themselves."

Suddenly Alan plunged his hand deep into his

pocket and brought it out with a laugh of relief. He showed Bart the silver dollar in his palm. "For a minute I was afraid I might've lost it."

"See," grinned Gordon. "I told you it was a lucky charm. Just you hang on to it."

The effort to reach Alan's mother by phone was useless. And the club steward told them that two of the big railroad stations had been badly bombed and no trains were running.

"Okay, tell you what," Bart said briskly. "My car's garaged a short way from here. I'll get it and we'll drive out in no time."

Ten minutes later, with Gordon at the wheel, Alan and his father were crowding into the front seat when a strange whistle made them wince. A second later, a bomb, jettisoned by a Nazi plane in trouble, crashed behind the club building. Glass from the upper windows tinkled onto the pavement beside the car.

Bart cried, "Holy cow! That was a close one. I hope you didn't have anything valuable in your club locker, Dave."

And in almost the same breath, Alan shouted, "My new boots! We left them here when we went to the docks."

David Lyons was already out of the car, running

up the steps. He came back quickly with the package containing the forgotten shoes and the information that the bomb had torn up the garden in the back but had hurt no one.

Bart Gordon threw the car impatiently into gear. Following whatever road was open, he had

worked his way some miles out through Epsom and Dorking by ten o'clock. Alan sat sleepily between the two men, half aware of the mutter of airborne engines and the crisscrossing of searchlight beams.

"Poor Maggie," he sighed, after a time.

"I suppose there are many Maggies in London, wondering how much more they can stand tonight," Mr. Lyons replied thoughtfully. But Alan roused himself enough to protest, "Maggie isn't wondering about how much *she* can stand."

And Bart agreed. "I'm doggone sure she isn't!"

It was midnight when the car sped at last into the placid, dark lanes of Middle Pentworth. Bart turned into the drive, Sireen yelped a welcome, and the door of the Lyons' house flew open.

Alan's mother, Cicely, and Mrs. Plume stood in the darkened doorway, faintly lit by the hooded headlights of the car, waiting only to be sure who was in it.

And then occurred one of the curious episodes of this uncertain period of the Battle of Britain.

Suddenly, distant churchbells began to toll, and were joined at once by the brassy clang from their own big village church and then the lesser clatter from the chapel. From every hamlet over the encircling downs there echoed the muted, swinging rhythms of big and little church bells.

It was the decreed government warning that a German invasion by sea had begun!

The men leaped from Bart Gordon's car, pushed

[*117*]

aside the frisking Sireen, and stood a moment, mystified.

"What a funny time for the invasion!" Bart said.

Already footsteps were pounding past the house as village men hurried, hastily dressed, toward the wardens' center.

Cicely clung to her father, but he said, "Run inside now, Sis, till I get back. I can't imagine what this means, Grace. All of you stay indoors, and I'll be home as soon as I know what's happening."

He ran to the house for his ARP helmet.

In the entryway he was confronted by Dickie Plume, half awake, his large, moist face stern. "Is this *it*, sir?" he demanded. "Are the Nazis attacking by sea?" Without waiting for an answer, he swung around and clattered upstairs.

Helmet in hand, Mr. Lyons ran out and found that Bart had started his motor, saying, "I'll go with you."

As the car screeched in a U-turn, Mrs. Plume pursed her lips. "Well, 'Itler or no 'Itler, I'm sure we'll all 'ave time for a nice cup a' tea," she declared and started toward the kitchen.

In the almost silent house, with Cicely curled up on the sofa and Sireen watchful at her feet, Alan sat beside his mother and began to recount his experiences of the afternoon. Mrs. Plume came in with a tower of thick sandwiches and pots of cocoa and tea.

"No word about the invasion?" she asked.

"The men haven't come back yet," the children's mother said. "We'll know then—" She paused with a look of alarm. *"What on earth's that?"*

There had been a loud clump at the head of the stairs. Mrs. Plume advanced to the newel post and looked up.

"Dickie," she said, unruffled. "You're ready, I see. Good. I expect Bottley'll be glad o' yer 'elp."

The confused medley of rattling metal, squeaking leather, and the clump of heavy boots started down the steps. Ole Dickie reached the bottom and turned.

"I'm orf," he stated briskly. "We licked them dunderheads once, and no reason we won't lick 'em again."

"Of course we shall, Dickie," Mrs. Lyons agreed. "You look ready for anything."

Wearing his World War I helmet, and outfitted with bayonet, canteen, torch, and an old hunting gun, Dickie clanked out the door and off up the dark street.

But it was no more than twenty minutes before

*"We licked them dunderheads once, and **no** reason we won't lick 'em again."*

David Lyons and Bart returned. The church bells, they reported, had given a false alarm. Somewhere in the great network of London's defense system, some nervous and over-anxious official had heard the code word "Cromwell"—which meant "PLACE ALL DEFENSE FORCES ON ALERT"—and had excitedly mistaken it for the signal which was to tell the British people that the German Operation Sea Lion had been launched. So swiftly did the nation's alarm devices work that before the mistake could be cancelled, all the church bells on the south coast had rung out.

Mrs. Plume's reaction startled the others, who heard the news with immeasurable relief. "Dickie *will* be disappointed," she said. " 'E was so lookin' for'ard to the fighting."

But Mr. Lyons said, "Wait, Mrs. Plume. Sergeant Bottley wants him to take on a special job. Do you think Mr. Plume can teach the Home Guard men expert rifle shooting?"

"Aow!" Mrs. Plume sat up with suddenly renewed vigor. *"Ov* course 'e can. You mean teach Whitty and them other bumblewits 'ow ter shoot when the Germans do come? A sharpshooter onct, a sharpshooter allus, I sye."

"So do I, Mrs. Plume," said Mrs. Lyons.

It was nearly two o'clock before Alan, scrubbed and drowsy with thick hot soup and treacle pudding, stumbled into bed. No one had wanted to leave the sitting room until Dickie returned. But he entered the house much more quietly than he had left, and minus most of the trappings he had worn.

"Come and have some soup, Dickie," Mrs. Lyons called when he paused, smiling shyly, at the door. "And tell us what happened."

"This 'ere war 'as its problems, ma'am," he began comfortably. "But me and Bottley'll 'andle that orl right, Bottley says, if I can teach Alf Whitty 'ow ter pull a trigger wivout jamming 'is ruddy thumb. I'm starting t'morrer, and 'e'll ruddy well learn afore I'm through." He fumbled about his empty web belt. "Feel nekked wivout me gear," he added. "Bottley said they needed all such."

Plumey rose hastily to her feet and declared, "Yer'd better get some sleep," and hurried him out of the room.

"By golly," yawned Bart Gordon. "I'll sleep better nights with men like that around."

CHAPTER NINE

Peter Joins Churchill's "Few"

ALAN came down to breakfast late next morning, and found his father and Bart at the table with their heads in the morning papers.

"Do they say how bad the second raid on London was last night?" Alan asked.

"Worse than the bombing we saw, in a way," his father replied. "Sent a lot of the fires *entirely* out of control. It destroyed tons of munitions from the U. S. and killed and hurt a lot of people. It also damaged the docks so badly it will take a long time to rebuild them."

"What about ports like Plymouth, and Liverpool, and Glasgow?" Alan asked, and Bart answered, "They'll be catching it hard, soon enough. The War Office seems to think last night's raid may mean the start of an all-out effort to knock Britain out by *air attack* alone."

Then Alan, remembering the scene after last midnight, asked, "Where's Dickie?"

"Mrs. Plume says he went out before six this morning," his father said. "I don't suppose any more boots will get polished in this house until he gets those 'bumblewits,' as she calls them, trained to shoot. The way the war news looks, we'll need every one of our Home Guard men."

The discussion was interrupted by the arrival of Rod, who started playing see-if-you-can-tear-off-my-sleeve with Sireen.

Rod hadn't exactly given up feeling that Alan was getting the best of things, but he had swallowed his own pride enough to be willing to accept Alan's excitement if he couldn't get in on things first-hand. He had already listened to a quick outline of Alan's trip to London from Dickie, whom he'd met marching Alf Whitty and the village black-smith out to the firing range.

His first words to Alan were: "You must lead a charmed life, boy, always on the spot when the Jerries start somep'in."

Alan fished Bart Gordon's good-luck coin from his pocket, held it out, and said, "I do."

"Doggone!" Rod exclaimed, in his best American manner. "Some charm! It's just a U. S. dollar, though, isn't it?"

"Oh, it's got plenty of rasmataz," Alan retorted, using one of Bart's expressions. "Anyway, it seems to work. What d'ya think a charm is? An Indian idol's eye or a voodoo doll?"

Gordon decided to return to town early that Sunday. The radio had been kept on all day, and the reports of the bombing that came over were menacing. Not long after he left, word was spread that another raid on London had begun, although not quite as heavy a one as on the previous day.

That Sunday slipped into the new week, and the weeks became a matter of steeling oneself to the dreadful raids that had become a daily pounding on Britain's beloved and stately London.

The promise of a break in the routine life of Middle Pentworth came one day when Alan announced to Rod that his brother, Peter, was coming home for a three-day leave with Dubbs O'Neil —"an old friend of mine I met in a kinda strange way at Dunkirk."

Rod was on hand at the railway station when Alan and his father went to meet the two fliers in trim, Air Force blue uniforms.

This was Alan's first meeting with Dubbs O'Neil since he had picked the Canadian out of the Channel.

The boy grinned self-consciously at the young pilot.

"Sure glad to see you again," O'Neil said. "I began to wonder whether I ever would. You got me out of a really nasty situation that night."

Peter and Dubbs felt almost giddy finding themselves free of flying duty for the first time since the Blitz—the London part of the Battle of Britain—began, and everything amused them. This included Sireen, who met them at the gate, delirious with joy at the thought of having so many new sleeves and trousers to tear.

That evening, over the biggest steak-and-kidney pie that Plumey had ever turned out, Alan admired O'Neil's Distinguished Flying Cross ribbon, awarded by the King.

Dubbs, a short, stocky young fellow with a soft voice, overheard Cicely ask Alan why O'Neil had a medal and Peter none. With a glint in his eye, Dubbs explained, "Well, missie, it looks as if King George thought I looked too plain even for a Colonial, and the Queen said, 'Maybe he'd be improved by a nice bit of jewelry.' So they gave me this."

Peter hooted. "Don't believe a word of that, sis. If I ever bring down as many Jerries as Dubbs has, they may give me one like it."

Baths, sleep, and almost unbroken bouts of

eating Plumey's good meals occupied a great deal of the young airmen's time for the next two days. On the second evening Alan, his father, mother, and Cicely lounged in comfortable chairs listening to the fliers' stories.

Dubbs excused himself and ran up to his room. When he came back, he said, "I'm returning your sweater," and tossed it to Alan.

Peter, toasting his feet at the library fire, glanced

up and remarked loudly, "Boy! are you lucky to get *that* back!"

"Well, it's Rod's sweater, not mine," Alan said slowly, holding it up to look with some awe at a long, singed rent in the back that had not been there when he had given it to O'Neil at Dunkirk. "This looks like a bullet hole or something."

Peter laughed. "Or something is right, Alan. That hole was made by a cannon shell. O'Neil had that sweater on when it happened. Tell him, Dubbs."

"Well, it turned out all right, at that." Dubbs O'Neil grinned at Alan.

"It was the first day the Jerries came over the

docks," Dubbs began. "Peter and I were on alert duty when the warning sounded in our dispersal hut. It's always a scramble to get to the planes in a hurry, but this time somebody yelled that the Jerries were coming over in shoals, and we really tore out to the flight line. The mechanics had our engines turning over before we got to 'em. On the way up to twenty thousand feet our Controller gave us the compass course to intercept the Jerries and we were in business.

"I had a little cold that day and was wearing the sweater. We spotted the Jerries coming in right away. We'd never seen so many before—hundreds of bombers with Messerschmitt 109's above and below.

"There were thirty-six of us from Biggin Hill. I was leading Red section in our squadron—six planes. Peter was in Blue section.

"We dived in among the Jerry bombers—twin-engined Dorniers with Messerschmitt fighters above them. I figured we might knock off a few bombers before their fighters could stop us, and I called on my Red Three and Four to follow me. I pulled up under one of the Dorniers, and gave him one short machine-gun burst.

"Luckily, I got a hit. He rolled over on his back,

with one engine on fire, and I saw him go down. So far, my wing man was sticking close to me."

Dubbs gestured with his hands, backs of the palms level to show how they had zoomed upward. "And we barged right down the middle of the Nazi formation. We got through, and I started looking for the Messerschmitts. Saw them coming down vertically at us, and I half-rolled around to get one more crack at the Dorniers—they'd scattered a little. I got one in my sights and I know I knocked some bits off the fuselage behind his rear gunner."

Peter broke in again impatiently. "Oh, I say! Nobody can get an idea of what a dog fight's like if you leave out the bit about guns blazing all over the place, and all that."

"Right," said Dubbs. "You've done it. Guns blazing and all that—"

"Didn't he go down—the second Dornier you hit?" Alan asked.

"I was too busy to watch whether he did or not," Dubbs admitted. "Right then, I felt some shots hit my tail, and when I looked back, my wing man wasn't there. But a Jerry fighter was, firing at me from an angle. Doggone sky was full of planes. I saw the 'L' painted on Peter's Spitfire, and I almost collided with another Jerry. I remember noticing Peter was after a Dornier, and another ship—I don't know whether it was theirs or ours—spinning down in flames.

"You have to remember these things all happen at once. I heard Red Four yelping for help in my earphones. He had two Jerries after him down below me, and I went after one of them. This fellow didn't see me, and I took off one wing with my first burst. That gave Red Four a chance to get the other Messerschmitt. You should have heard what he yelled when that Jerry pilot bailed out." O'Neil paused self-consciously.

"Just skip what he said," Alan's father suggested. "We have an idea."

O'Neil continued, "By that time the Nazi bombers were unloading. I saw fires start all along the river, and I was blazing mad."

"And soon after that," Peter broke in, "we chased the bombers past Southend and found ourselves over the North Sea. That's where O'Neil got his. Tell 'em how, lad."

Dubbs grinned. "I had my eye on the Dorniers above me, until suddenly I discovered four ME's trying to box me in. They thought I was a sitting duck, but I didn't think so. I had one of them lined up in my gunsight—when all at once there was a horrible thudding noise back of my seat. I felt a crease sting my back, and glass from the canopy-cover and bits of broken instruments began to clatter around like hail.

"Then my engine began to run rough. I dived into some cloud cover and wondered what the blazes I was going to do. My radio'd been knocked out, and I couldn't raise the Biggin Hill Control for a heading to get myself back home. I began to figure I'd have to bail out, even if I was over water. I tried to slide open the cockpit cover to jump. But it'd been jammed when one of the cannon shots hit it. I couldn't believe the ship'd hold together too long, but there was nothing to do *but* ride her down."

Peter shivered sympathetically, and Cicely piped up anxiously, "What happened to those German planes all around you?"

Dubbs chuckled, lit a fresh cigarette, and sat back living over those moments in his mind. "I *had* to come out of the clouds to see where I was, Sis, and the Jerries had disappeared. I nursed the poor old kite over the coast and then discovered that the landing wheels were jammed, too."

"However, when I flew over Biggin Hill at dusk

[*133*]

they could see that I was in trouble, and had fire trucks and an ambulance lined up by the time I'd circled. Never thought I'd be glad to see an ambulance waiting. I didn't need it, though. Made a belly-landing with all my switches off, and the fire boys got me out of that crate faster'n you could open a sardine can.

"Handing that sweater over to you's the end of the story, Alan. The hole's where the cannon shot grazed my back. Bad luck for your friend's sweater, but I was barely nicked."

"Rod'll *like* to have that hole in his sweater, I expect, seeing how it got there," said Alan.

It was always lonely at Holmewood when Peter went back after a leave, but it was worse this time, because the fliers' visit had reflected the excitement and high spirits they felt.

It had become plain to the world at the end of 1940 that the German High Command was trying to completely destroy the country's morale. All that winter Goering sent the Luftwaffe out in heavy attacks on industrial and other targets, challenging the outnumbered British Air Force to come up and be destroyed. But, although it had losses, the RAF air defence was not shattered. Its radar spotted the oncoming enemy, and had been so improved that the element of surprise attack **was** greatly reduced. Savage as the bombings were, **the** British bore them with stubborn bravery.

Hitler was infuriated by the failure to subdue the British, since he wanted to be free to attack Russia. Every military expert said this could not be done until England collapsed. The German High Command was ready to agree to any kind of terror action that would bring the British to their knees, so the massive attacks continued. And with hundreds of other Colonial and English youths, Peter and O'Neil shot up into the skies at each onslaught. They blazed away, with a growing sense of confidence, at the Nazi air fleets.

Toward spring O'Neil was moved off to an Operational Training Unit to pass his skills on to fledgling pilots. And Peter came home one day and asked his mother to sew an additional stripe on his uniforms. He had been given O'Neil's job and the rank of Flight Lieutenant.

Alan's map in the library had become what Cicely called a silly mess. Red marks indicating German victories had been drawn farther and farther across it—crossing off conquered Greece and the Balkans, where Hitler's Italian partner, Mussolini, had marched in with German help.

"The Italian armies are also down here in Egypt," Alan explained.

Cicely peered at the map more closely. "But *look,* Alan." She frowned. "The Germans are going farther and farther *away* from England. That's *good,* isn't it?"

"Didn't you hear the radio news last night?" Alan demanded. "The bomb raids on us were just as bad as ever."

"Well," retorted Cicely, "Peter's always shooting German planes down. What I don't see is where all the German pilots are coming from. Maybe they'll give out soon."

A year had passed since Sireen put in his first grubby appearance, and no one mentioned Oklahoma any more. A new green spring at last brought pleasant weather. Plumey aired out the Anderson hut, Mrs. Lyons planted flowers around it, and the family enjoyed being outdoors again. Alan felt that although the defense of Britain was proceeding wonderfully well, life in Middle Pentworth was going sort of stale.

And then Bart Gordon set it topsy-turvy with a different kind of bombshell.

"Will you please get Alan and Cicely ready to sail for New York?" he phoned.

CHAPTER TEN

Oklahoma Bound

ALAN and Cicely's trip to America had been talked about so long that when the children and their parents were actually faced with the decision, it seemed like an entirely new calamity.

"I'll never see you and Daddy again," Cicely wailed to her mother. And Alan stuck out his lower lip and asked stubbornly, "Why *should* we go? I don't want to run away from whatever's going to happen at home, Dad."

Their parents did not tell them that the thought of the Atlantic crossing, when two ships carrying British children to America had already been torpedoed, was agonizing.

No one knew, that spring, how long the war would last. But Mr. and Mrs. Lyons, having seen how Alan managed to find himself under fire, were inclined to agree with Bart Gordon that sending them to America was wise.

Cicely spent the next few days glumly washing, combing, and petting Sireen, enjoying, against her better judgment, the new clothes her mother got her, interrupted by spells of throwing herself on members of the family, chanting protests.

"But darling," her mother said, "you won't be away too long, probably. And perhaps Daddy and I may come to Oklahoma and bring you back. I'd love that. Wouldn't you?"

Looking up from under her tousled hair, Cicely asked suspiciously, "How soon?"

However, saying good-by at school did give both Cicely and Alan a feeling of being on the verge of a special adventure.

Bart had worked out a simple timetable for the start of the journey. Their father would bring the children to London and say good-by there. Bart Gordon would take them on by train to Glasgow, Scotland, from which port their ship would sail. In Glasgow, he would place them under the care of a Miss Talbott, secretary in an American Government agency. She had finished her work in the Scotland office and was returning to New York. "She's a

good, steady person," Gordon told Mrs. Lyons.
"I've seen her on business matters several times
while I've been here."

The ship was to sail May 9th, and passengers
were to be at the embarkation port on the preced-
ing evening.

Plumey grew steadily more mournful as she
thought of all the things the children faced. Serv-
ing Cicely's favorite raspberry trifle, she said, "Eat
this up, duckie, and I'll bring yer more. 'Eaven
knows wot them Okly'omer Indians eat."

Early on the morning of the 8th, Ole Dickie
hauled the bulging valises downstairs and trun-
dled them off to the station in his barrow. Sireen
spent a good deal of time getting stepped on, and
being comforted. Breakfast was over, articles the
children were to carry were laid out in the entrance
hall. A list was being checked, in case anything
had been forgotten, and Plumey took advantage of
the confusion to cram a package of sweet biscuits
into Alan's coat pocket.

The doorbell rang.

Mr. Lyons opened the door. Sergeant Bottley
and a stranger with one arm in a sling stood there.
Plunging through the open door, Sireen danced
around the sergeant. Alan snatched at his collar.

But before he caught it, the stranger knelt down beside the dog and said, "How're you, boy!" To everyone's astonishment the dog's yelps suddenly changed tone. Jumping up with little high-pitched cries, he began to lick the caller's free hand and face frantically.

"That's my pup," the stranger said, smiling up at the policeman. "That's him, all right."

Sergeant Bottley looked about the group guiltily.

"This gentleman is Mr. Art 'Arris," he said. "Ye remember, sir, that a pup o' this description ran away when the Emsworth 'ouse was bombed? It's a real shyme ye've all got so attached to the animal. Mr. 'Arris 'ere is only just now out of 'orspital."

Alan waited in shocked silence, and his father said politely to the stranger, "I'm glad to see you've recovered, sir. The dog certainly seems to know you, doesn't he?"

And just then Cicely, starched and gloved for travel, burst through the door. Alan, in the hope that breaking the news to her himself would make it less painful, said hastily, "Sis, this is the man whose house was bombed and his dog ran away. Well, it seems Sireen really is his dog. See, Sireen remembers him."

Cicely studied Sireen, who was now wriggling

happily in the stranger's arms. Tenderness and her recent end-of-the-world feeling battled in her heart. Suddenly she said to the man, "Well, I sup-

pose if you *love* him you can take him back."

The stranger bowed. "Thanks, miss. My wife Ellie *will* be grateful to you for giving him up.

She's just come from the hospital too, and having the pup again'll do her a world a' good."

"You're welcome," Cicely replied primly, and gently kissed Sireen good-by on his forehead.

The callers and the dog went off. The children's father said, "I'm proud of you both."

But Cicely had stretched fair play too far. "I hate him, I hate him, I *hate* him," she cried and threw herself on her father in a tornado of tears.

Alan mumbled soothingly, "It's better to give him up quickly. You saw how happy Sireen was, Sis." And her father urged, "Come on, now. We must be getting along, or we'll miss that train."

Their mother had stood miserably inside the door watching the unexpected little parting, thinking, "This is really too much." However, she pulled herself together and called out cheerfully, "They're leaving, Plumey. Come and say good-by."

In this air of bustle, the family separated without the expected storm.

In spite of herself, Cicely, who had not visited London often, was already beginning to feel guiltily excited. She thereupon fell into a sort of numbed silence, her large blue eyes rolling to take in everything on the train ride, then bomb-damaged Victoria Station, and the strangeness of London.

Afterwards, in the taxi across town Bart Gordon took her small gloved hand in his enormous warm grasp. She held his hand tightly, and on the other side, her father's, and stared from the window at the blackened, glassless skeletons of buildings, and the hurrying, cheerful throngs passing by almost without noticing the wreckage.

In their compartment, moving out of the King's Cross Railway station, she and Alan watched the figure of their father drift backwards as the train pulled out and headed for Scotland. On the long trip north Bart Gordon repeated the detailed instructions they were to follow when they arrived in New York. Mrs. Gordon would meet the ship, but in case she missed them, he told them where to go.

"But you shouldn't have any trouble," he said. "Miss Talbott will see to everything."

From the train they watched the countryside glide by—old towns, smoke curling upward from camouflaged factory chimneys, soldiers everywhere, and later the soft, rolling hills and moors of Scotland.

On the early evening drive through Glasgow from the Queen Street Station to the hotel, Cicely fell asleep. Alan asked Bart innumerable questions about the city, the shipyards on the Clyde, and the not too distant airfield at Prestwick where the transatlantic planes came in.

They found Miss Talbott waiting for them in the lobby, and both children instantly took a positive dislike to her.

She was a stocky, plain woman, with rather bony jaws and a smile that flitted on and off automatically. "Oh, there you are, dearies," she said. "I'm sure we're going to have all sorts of fun." Then she put a hand over her mouth, bent her sensibly hatted head toward Bart, and whispered loudly, "If we get through those German submarine wolf-packs."

Bart frowned. "Miss Talbott. I wouldn't be sending these children off if I thought it was as bad as that. You'll get across all right."

Miss Talbott started to speak but closed her mouth again, and looked uneasily at her charges.

"I really don't know much about children's habits," she said.

"Well," Bart Gordon drawled, "*one* of their habits is to go to bed early when they've had a long, hard day—and that's now." He arranged for dinner to be sent up to their rooms.

Bart felt sorry somehow for the kids. Miss Talbott didn't show up here as well as she did over an office desk. But she's okay, he thought. He kissed Cicely, and said to Alan, "Tell you what, son, I have to attend a meeting over at the air station tonight. But I'll be back by nine in the morning to take you to the ship. After that I've got to go back to Prestwick for two-three days, and I'll send your dad word as soon as you've sailed. Okay?"

He handed the children's passports, money, and other documents to their guardian, and called, "Toodle-oo." Throwing a kiss back to Cicely, he swung through the street door and went out to a waiting Air Force car.

Alan was by now quite sure that neither he nor Cicely could endure the idea of going on with the trip. Miss Talbott only made the unwelcome voyage seem more unbearable than it had been before. This resolution was strengthened by the dreadful face Cicely made at him and the sparkle of tears in her eyes as she followed Miss Talbott into their bedroom. Shut in his own room, after eating, he sat glowering at the strange carpet for a long time. But what could he do? He and Cicely were trapped.

He had not yet undressed when the familiar wail of sirens echoed down the dusky streets.

Miss Talbott shot through the door between the rooms, ordering, in a rising tone, "Put on something warm," and *"Come,* Cicely, there's no time to dawdle. The shelter's way down in the cellar," all in one breath.

Cicely, in a thick coat over her clothes, stood in a majestic rage, as Alan went to fetch her. "She's scared as a rabbit," Cicely hissed triumphantly. But Alan just said, "Never mind, we've got to do as

she says," and shepherded Cicely downstairs with the other guests.

Settled in the safety of the underground concrete cubicle, and surrounded by calm companions, Miss Talbott relaxed and chatted agreeably —pausing only when the thud of a bomb strike near the hotel shook the earth. She nodded at the sleeping Cicely, and leaning away from Alan, said to the old Scotsman beside her, "Their par-

POLICE — DANGER

ents want to get them out of England before the country falls. Very wise, I—"

She jerked back open-mouthed as the Scotsman rose to his feet and said icily, "Madame, nae guid Briton'd think a' sech a thing."

Only Alan's rigid training in mannerly behavior toward his elders prevented his sputtering out the words that surged through his mind. Instead he said, "My parents don't believe Britain can be beaten by anybody, Miss Talbott. I think you misunderstood."

Miss Talbott stared at him, unbelieving. When the "All Clear" came, she crept with the children upstairs to their rooms, feeling drained of what courage she once had.

She woke the children at dawn. "We'll have to get to the ship before there's another raid," she said. "After that one last night, I don't know what's left of the streets. We can't wait for Mr. Gordon. We'll have breakfast, and then run."

Alan protested, "But we *must* see him again." However, Miss Talbott reminded Alan tartly that they had been put in her charge and Mr. Gordon himself had told them to do exactly what she ordered—for their own safety.

The loquacious taximan who drove them to

nearby Gourock, where the ship lay, told them all about the damage done to the city in the night's "tip and run" raid.

Miss Talbott had aroused Cicely to a fit of rebellion unlike her usual gentle self. Following Miss Talbott up the gangway to the ship's deck, Cicely hung behind and whispered to Alan, "She's really horribly awful, isn't she?" And Alan, with doom settling farther down on his head with every step, agreed. "She's a blithering idiot."

Seamen and various officials closed in around them, and there was everywhere the distraction of the whistling ships and the tooting barges.

The first passengers to arrive, Miss Talbott and the children went along the narrow inner passage smelling of food and oily bilge-water. When their baggage was stowed away in the little cabins, she said they might go back on deck for a breath of air. There they were watching the last of the cargo being hoisted aboard, when suddenly another raid warning sounded.

Alan grabbed Cicely's hand. "Alan!" she shouted. "Where do we go now?"

"I don't know, Sis," Alan whispered excitedly, "but the point is to *go*. Maybe this is our chance to get away!"

CHAPTER ELEVEN

A Moment of History

FOR a few seconds after the warning, stevedores, officers, and seamen stood scanning the sky above the tall masts and dock cranes. Then, off in the direction of Glasgow, guns began to boom, and the men on ship and dock began to shout and run to their stations. The muzzle of an anti-aircraft gun on the stern of their ship tilted skyward, its helmeted crew springing to action.

Feet pounded along the decks. An officer noticed the children alone and told them sternly where to find shelter near the dock entrance. "Go, as fast as ye can," he commanded.

Alan and Cicely ran down the gangway. They zigzagged through the shed piled high with cargo, and continued on *past* the dock air-raid shelter to which they had been directed. Overhead the drone of approaching aircraft drummed increasingly louder.

"Where *are* we going, Alan?" Cicely puffed. "I'm frightened."

"You can't stop to be frightened now," he said fiercely. "Come *along,* past these piers. There'll be *somewhere* to duck into— *Sprint,* can't you!"

They successfully evaded the hand of a tall, sandy Scottish policeman who shouted to them, "In hererr, bairrns, the shelterrr's here!" He stared in a bewildered way as they lunged out of his reach.

Some yards farther on, Alan glanced over his shoulder to see how near the bombers had come. A vast hand clamped on his shoulder, swung him about, and another hand caught Cicely. A huge, A.R.P. man said gruffly, "In you go to this shelter —here. No need to be scared. There, *now,* missy, no tricks."

Cicely struggled, but he picked her up and strode quickly to an ancient stone building and thrust her through the door, pushing Alan in after her.

The twenty minutes spent in the dank cellar among long, dim rows of huge barrels gave Alan time to think. He whispered to Cicely, "Now, Sis, if you want to go back to the ship, we'll go. But if we try, we can find Bart Gordon and make him understand we'd much rather go home. Are you willing to take a chance? You say."

Cicely gave him her kitten smile.

"Okay." He grinned back. "But you've got to do exactly what I say, understand?" Cicely nodded.

Alan continued. "When the door opens we'll slip out beside that fat couple, and you skitter off as fast as you can."

Their escape, after the "All Clear" opened the doors, proved very simple. Before the warden missed them they were around the corner and running up a cobbled slope. About a quarter of a mile farther, Cicely said, "These stones hurt my feet terribly horribly," and Alan said encouragingly, "It'll be safe now to ask for a ride." He signaled to a driver turning out from a shipyard, who drew up and called, "Want a lift?"

It was an old truck loaded with iron castings and the driver a plain, ruddy-faced countryman. The children climbed up.

Alan explained that they wanted to get to Prestwick to meet a family friend. The driver said he thought he could get them a good step along the way, and from the place where he turned off they could pick up a bus.

The instant the siren sounded, Miss Talbott, sitting on the edge of her berth, let out a cry of exasperation. "Oh, not again!" She noticed a uniformed figure hurrying past her cabin door and called sharply, "Officer, what are we supposed to do?"

He paused to smile reassuringly. "Just get off the ship as quickly as you can, ma'am. There's a shelter near." He paused politely to see that she was really going to leave.

Miss Talbott began to search hurriedly for something among her possessions, and scolded, "I can't find my handbag, and it has everything I own in it as well as— OH! THE CHILDREN!"

"What children, ma'am?"

"A boy and a girl. I let them go on deck," she wailed.

To the officer's ears the sound of metal doors clanging, barked commands, swift footsteps, and the screech of machinery swivelling into action meant that they must get clear of the ship at once.

Spotting her handbag, the officer grabbed it and hurried Miss Talbott to the deck in a state verging on panic. From the top of the gangway, she looked anxiously out over the heads of the crowd below, and some distance off she caught sight of Alan and Cicely.

"There they are—the children, thank heaven! Stop them!"

"Stop who? Oh, no, ma'am. You just catch up with them. The warden posted at the gate will tell you where to go."

Hurriedly she set off with the throngs being herded along.

She had gone only a few yards when she heard her name shouted. Bart Gordon, flinging himself out of a taxi, pushed his way toward her.

"Where are Alan and Cicely?" he shouted.

"They *were* on deck, perfectly all right, till this alarm," she cried. "I saw them just up ahead."

Gordon took her arm and all but lifted her along to the shelter entrance indicated by the warden. By this time the crash of bombs in the distance was lost in the drone of planes overhead diving toward the docks. Detonations burst nearer, and anti-aircraft guns roared a fierce tattoo. Shrapnel clattered on the roofs and the pavement.

Gordon dragged his companion into the shelter and looked around. The vaulted cellar was low and dim, but the people were in small, easily observed groups.

"Alan and Cicely aren't here!" he fumed. "Miss Talbott, how *could* you let them get out of your sight?"

Before poor Miss Talbott could answer, he bounded back up the steps only to run into the steely grasp of a large Scottish bobby with a granite chin and icily reproving blue eyes. "Y'er gaeing nowheres, Meester Boock Rogers. *Git doon,*" he ordered.

"I've got to find two children who're in my charge," Gordon replied testily. "Have you seen them? A boy fourteen and a girl about ten?"

"Well, now, and I did, a few minutes back," the bobby replied after a moment. "They slipped rrright oota me hands. Likely the big officer doon the rrroad stowed them in the beerrr vault they've turrrned into a shelterrr."

Wondering why the children had not come into this nearest shelter, Gordon leaned back against the wall, fretting.

The Scotsman's last words were lost in a terrific explosion. The ground and building shook, but a following blast sounded much farther away. In another fifteen minutes the "All Clear" came. The moment the bobby stood aside, Gordon bolted out. He knew where the old beer vault was, and ran up the roadway toward it.

A minute later Miss Talbott came up to Gordon standing at the door of the vault shelter talking to an A.R.P. man. Both were glowering.

"Sure, I put them in here when they came along," the man snapped. "Had to pick up the lass and carry her. No, I didn't see them come out. After all—"

"Okay," snapped Bart. "Skip it. You did your duty. Come on, Miss Talbott. They may have gone to another shelter. If not, I'll send out a police alarm."

But within an hour it was certain that Alan and Cicely had not returned to the ship or to the hotel. Nor had they been seen at any railway or bus station. A description of them and a pick-up order had begun to travel from Police Headquarters in Glasgow to sub-stations in all neighboring villages and towns. Miss Talbott sat apprehensive in her cabin, and Gordon walked the Clydeside, returning to the ship at intervals.

Soon after lunch he boarded the liner for the last time and waited glumly until three o'clock when he was told he'd have to go ashore. Miss Talbott, in tears, returned the money, passports, and baggage placed in her charge, which Gordon transported to the hotel. Then he telephoned Mr. and Mrs. Lyons at Holmewood.

While Alan and Cicely rumbled away out of

the shipping area, the driver kept up a steady chatter about the heavy enemy raids, but in a broad dialect of which they understood only part. Alan let the old fellow's comments about the two of them traveling by themselves pass without answering, and the driver grinned. He had, he said, nine childer of his own, and blest if he knew where they kept theirselves most of the time, what wi' fishin' and scoorin' the lanes. . . .

Alan put his mind to two problems he had to solve. One was that Miss Talbott had all their cash, which meant they had no bus fare nor money for anything else. And he recalled suddenly that, since the beginning of the war, all road signs had been removed. He began to wonder whether it was going to be as easy as he'd thought to find Prestwick.

They drew up in a small town, and the driver said, "This is Kilbarchan, where I turn off. But I've got to get me a wee bite here in this tavern. Will ye no join me?"

When Alan said, "Oh, no, thank you," Cicely pinched his arm, and he let his protests die. He was glad he had when the big plates of delicious-smelling food were put in front of them.

On parting, the Scotsman pointed out the bus stop from which they could get transportation to a place called Busby, where another bus would take them to Prestwick.

He then went home and milked his cows. By so doing, he missed the radio news that two English children were being sought by the police.

Cicely put up a mild protest when she found that she was supposed to walk from there on. Alan figured that a bobby or a well-meaning stranger, seeing them, might ask uncomfortable questions about where they were going. The afternoon was warm, and the smell of heather on the air was sweet. Very shortly both were ambling happily along, letting cars that halted to ask whether they wanted a lift go off with a polite "No, thank you." During the afternoon Alan discovered Plumey's biscuits in his pocket, and they provided supper.

"We better not try to go on after dark," Alan said as twilight hovered. "We might get lost." And soon afterwards they came on a detached sheep cote lying in a quiet valley near a cool, noisy stream. The lofts were filled with clean hay, and they were surprised to find what a lovely bed it made.

It was chilly washing in the stream next morning after they had been wakened by the sun. But, aside from wishing they could tell their parents where they were, the sense of adventure in this beautiful unfamiliar Scottish countryside sent them off happily again—though very hungry.

They hadn't gone far when they saw a tiny stone house with smoke streaming from its chimney, set in a nest of the hillside, and a pleasant-looking woman near it drawing water from a well.

Hunger gnawed at their insides. "Would it be begging if we asked her to give us just a teeny breakfast?" Cicely asked.

Alan's eyes lit up suddenly. He rummaged in his pocket and extracted from it Gordon's silver dollar. "We can offer her this." He grinned. "After we get to Prestwick we won't need money."

The woman laughed when Alan offered her the American coin, and smoothed Cicely's blond hair. "Oh, I canna tak' yer money, laddie," she protested, "for a few mouthfuls of vittles. Let you come t'the spring hoose and help me bring the milk, and we'll hae a gude bite tegither." It was porridge and scones and several jugs of milk in the end that sent them along the road.

Alan was relaxed now. The ship had sailed without them.

During the day, he inquired of other country people and was told that he had taken the longest road to Prestwick, and he began to worry a little for fear of missing Gordon. The road they were following skirted the southern rim of Glasgow part of the way. The Duke of Hamilton's home, so a shepherd said, was not far off. By afternoon Alan wondered whether they would reach their goal by nightfall. By twilight he knew they wouldn't.

"Mummy will be worried sick," Cicely declared. "We ought to ask a policeman to telephone and tell her we're all right." Alan agreed but thought Bart should do it instead of the police.

"We'll keep on walking, but if we don't come to Prestwick soon, we'll ask a bobby for help," he decided.

And so they trudged on. A keeper with a gun eyed them over a farm wall, and when Alan asked whether they were headed right for Prestwick, he nodded, "Aye," and watched them out of sight.

Despite several halts to rest on the ferny roadside, as complete darkness fell Cicely began to whimper.

"Alan, this is ridiculous, and I've got a horrible blister," she complained.

"All right, Sis," Alan said. He had noticed, a little distance back, a haystack standing among the sloping fields not far from the road, and he led her to it. The hay was sweet, and they stretched out on the far side of the rick and fell asleep without taking off their shoes.

The countryside slumbered except for watchers posted in the small villages around—Busby, Eagelsham, and Mearns—where Army and civilian plane-spotters and Home Guard centers remained on a drowsy vigil.

The presence of Nazi planes in the skies was taken for granted. At any moment they might appear anywhere on the British landscape. Keeping track of their movements was the duty of the Observer Corps.

On this night, farm hands had made their last rounds and climbed into bed, and the almost full moon had risen and sailed swiftly upward through the drifting clouds.

Just before midnight, Cicely woke suddenly. A single plane very low overhead had aroused her. After listening a second, she reached out and tugged at her brother's arm. "Alan, Alan, wake up," she begged. "There's a plane coming down on us!"

Alan sat up instantly. The throb of the aircraft as it circled back over the roof of a farmhouse a short distance below them, brought him violently upright.

"It's a Messerschmitt 110!" he said in amazement. "What's he doing here? Their range is too short for a round trip from Germany. It can't *be*." It was silhouetted sharply by the moon. "But it is! It's a German ME-110!"

As they watched, the plane's engines stopped, and a moment later a parachute billowed out against the night sky. Below the chute something dangled from its shrouds.

"It's a landmine," Alan cried. "Lie flat!" He crouched, but with his head tipped to watch the chute's descent, and saw, in a moment, that the dangling object was a man.

"It's not a mine, Sis," he said more quietly. "It's a German airman. Maybe a spy."

At that moment, above the hillside they were on, the plane struck the ground with a shattering crash.

"Look," Cicely cried, pointing excitedly, "the man's going to land right near us."

Alan was too puzzled by the strangeness of the German's arrival to move. But as the chutist crumpled to the ground in a tangle of silk and shroud-lines, he began to run toward him.

"We must see who he is. Where are the police?" he exclaimed. Cicely set out after him, and they raced toward the slope on which the figure still sat enmeshed.

A light flared from the nearby farmhouse door, and now the pounding of feet came running up the hill. Alan pulled Cicely down beside some bracken to watch. The newcomer was obviously a farmer. He approached the figure and bent down to question him. Even from a distance Alan could see the pale, heavy-browed man on the ground grin and indicate that he couldn't get up. He was speaking English with a thick German accent.

"I haf hurt my leg," he said.

The Scotsman leaned down and helped him rise. "Ah'll take ye t'the cottage," he said, "and gie ye a coop o' tea."

Standing, the German was a tall, gaunt figure in high boots and the uniform of a Nazi officer. Alan wondered who he could be and what had prompted him to parachute to this remote Scottish farm. Because, although a British Defiant fighter plane had been in pursuit and had almost overtaken the ME-110, not a single shot had been fired!

The German leaned on the farmer, and they moved a little way toward the farmhouse and stopped. The German said that he'd like to have his parachute to keep. "It safed my life," he explained, and the farmer went back to scoop it up, then resumed the painful journey to the cottage.

Alan and Cicely followed slowly after them and stood where they could see inside. There was a middle-aged woman in the room and another man.

The German was eased to a seat beside the kitchen fireplace, and the motherly woman offered to make him tea. He said no, but he'd like a glass of water. All this time Alan was growing more disturbed. This was a matter for the police. Although he knew that the countryfolk were canny and not to be hoodwinked, he felt that time was being lost in notifying the authorities of the German's landing.

"What if there are other Nazis landing all over these hills, too?" he said, thinking aloud.

"Well," Cicely replied, "if there are, do we just stand here and let them?"

"Certainly not," Alan replied. "Where do you suppose the Home Guard is? There must be a station near here. We'd better go find it while those people keep him safe in there."

But as he spoke he heard more pounding footsteps and saw figures running down the road. Alan pulled Cicely into the shadow as two soldiers entered the farmhouse.

"Observer Corpsmen," one man explained at the door. And, watching through an open window, Alan saw that they were questioning the prisoner and noted that they were as puzzled as he was about the German's landing there.

"We spotted the Messerschmitt coming down and him parachuting out," Alan heard one say. "We couldn't believe our eyes. Even the RAF said we'd made a mistake in identification, that it wasn't an ME-110, *but we knew it was.*"

For a few minutes, uneasy whispering and a study of the prisoner went on, but this was interrupted shortly by the arrival of two Home Guardsmen in a car. Both wore steel helmets and what appeared to be hurriedly donned uniforms. One carried a first World War pistol.

Alan and Cicely had edged close to the door and then slipped silently within the shadow of the room. The firelight and oil lamp cast a dim, soft glow over the odd midnight spectacle.

The German had been found to be unarmed. He said that he was "Oberleutnant Horn" and

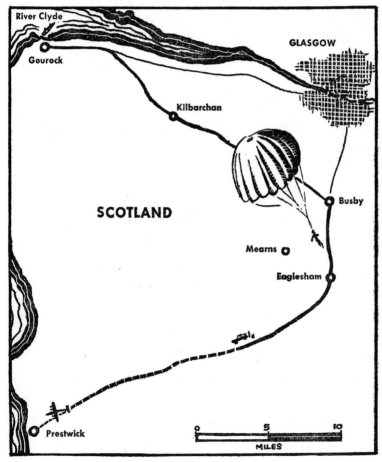

that he was alone. When questioned, he insisted that he had come to persuade important people in the government that England should make peace with the Nazis, and asked to see the Duke of Hamilton.

Cicely, who revered all the great names of Britain, whispered, "Oh! Alan, that's utter nonsense."

Alan had been studying the man closely. Still puzzled, he said softly, "Sis, that man's no ordinary flier—he's too old. He might be a whopping high-up Nazi."

As he talked, a photograph came slowly but more and more clearly to his mind.

It was a mystified group that helped the German out to the Home Guardsmen's car in which he was driven away. Alan and Cicely, who had scurried out of the room ahead of the others, now watched the car's departure from several yards off. When it had gone, they stumbled down the dark road to talk.

For the last few minutes Alan had become more excited. After the light went out in the cottage, he drew Cicely closer and said, "I *know* who that German is. I've got his picture at home. His name's not Oberleutnant Horn, as he said. It's Rudolf Hess! He's Hitler's right-hand man!"

CHAPTER TWELVE

The Luftwaffe Admits Defeat

CICELY, on whom the name *Hitler* had a terrifying effect, could not utter a sound.

"Another thing," Alan went on. "One of those Home Guard men noticed us. We'd better get to Bart Gordon fast."

Cicely no longer felt adventurous. She just wanted to get back to familiar things, to which Bart would be the first step. She needed no urging to start marching again.

The road led through softly sweeping country where only the uplands and the tops of slopes were lit by moonlight. They trudged past dark, slumbering stone houses and fields for nearly an hour. Occasionally an early-waking rooster crowed. They stopped to watch a four-engined transport letting down, engines throttled.

"That must be Prestwick where it's going to land, Cicely," Alan exclaimed. "It's not much farther."

Their attention was still fixed on its long glide in the distance when a car which they had not heard came around a bend in the road and screeched to a stop beside them. From it, the helmeted guardsman who had driven off with the German slid out, flashed a light in their faces, and said "Joost a minute, lad. Is ye name Alan Lyons?"

After a moment's hesitation, Alan said, "Yes, sir."

The policeman shouted back to the car, "It's them." And then to the boy, he queried, "D'ye ken there's an alarm out f'r ye—t'breeng y' home?"

"No, sir," Alan replied politely, "we didn't know. We are on our way to find a friend of our father's in Prestwick."

"Ye doon't say! I'm afraid we're going t'have t' take ye both back t' the station. We'll see ye find yer friend. Coom along noo."

The car with Alan and Cicely inside swung around in the direction from which it had come.

And so the adventure ended in the little Home Guard Station at Busby, where, not long before they arrived, "Oberleutnant Horn" had been officially turned over to the British Army for safe-keeping. And before Alan and Cicely had finished an early breakfast, supplied by the wardens, Bart Gordon walked in. He had arrived by borrowed car, too relieved on finding them unhurt to show how angry and alarmed he had felt.

Alan said feebly, "We're sorry to have upset everyone's plans, but—" and with a slight grin held up the silver dollar.

Bart interrupted brusquely, "I don't see that there's anything to do about what's past, now."

He then turned to the officer in charge and said, "Hear there was a little excitement around this station last night." But as soon as the men on duty had given a short summary of Oberleutnant Horn's capture, Gordon looked at his watch, and said they could just catch the ten o'clock train to London if they hurried.

Alan wanted to ask whether any of them knew who their Nazi prisoner was. But he decided if he told them it was Hess they'd laugh at him, and so remained silent.

"You'll find London fair bashed up, I fear," the chief said in parting. "More than five hundred bombers covered it the nicht, and two thousand incendiary canisters dropped."

On the train Bart buried himself in a Glasgow newspaper's account of London's latest and one of her heaviest raids, while his charges slept or stared at the landscape.

They should have arrived at Euston Station in London at five-fifteen that afternoon, but the destruction from the night before was widespread, and the train was shunted from track to track several times before it drew in.

On the taxi trip across town to the station from which they would take the local train home Alan saw how last night's bombing had ravaged the city.

The welcome that Cicely and Alan got when they arrived home was so temperate that her adventure lost the last of its thrill for Cicely. Her parents kissed her and told her coolly to have her supper and get right off to bed. And there was no Sireen to lavish wild affection on her and Alan. The worst cut was Plumey's curt greeting: "So yer back!" Cicely cried a little going up to bed, because she was very tired, and muttered, "Well, I'd rather be turned into an icicle than be on that ship to America."

For a time after his supper Alan sat slumped on the sofa listening to his father and Bart discussing not only last night's raid on London, but the odd account Bart had heard of a German officer who had parachuted into Scotland and asked to see the Duke of Hamilton. "The Duke represented that district in Parliament," Bart observed, "and now during the war is a Wing Commander in the RAF in charge of a fighter sector near Edinburgh. But why did this Nazi pick on him? No one in the countryside understands it."

Alan's father said to him, "I hear you were taken to the same Home Guard headquarters where they kept Oberleutnant Horn till the police turned him over to the Army."

Alan said, "Yes, we were," and wondered doubtfully: would they believe me if I told them who he really is? He had gone at once to look at his picture of Hess in the library again, and now he was sure.

"That German's name *isn't* Horn, though," he offered as a trial balloon.

"Obviously it isn't," his father stated without interest. But Bart took his pipe from his mouth and looked at him curiously. "Who do *you* think he is?"

Alan hesitated, flushed, and said in a rush, "Well, I *know* who he is, sir. We saw him face to face when he landed."

At this both men bolted upright and cried, "You what?" And Bart added irritably, "Why didn't one of you tell me coming down on the train?"

"You didn't ask us, sir," Alan replied, and hastily went on to explain, "When the Home Guard officer didn't tell you about seeing Cicely and me in the farmhouse, I wasn't sure you'd believe me if I told you we'd been there."

Then followed the story, and it wasn't until Alan had reached the end of his account that his father said, "Well, what makes you so sure you know who the parachutist was?"

Alan rose and got his map with the pictures of Nazi officers around its border. He pointed to the one of Rudolf Hess.

"You're kidding," said Bart. But his father looked at him long and speculatively. "It just might be," he grinned after a while. "Hess is the only Nazi of the lot except Hitler himself who'd think he might be able to persuade Britain to give up to Germany. It just could be."

Forty-five hours after the moonlight landing of "Oberleutnant Horn," the German wireless broadcast that Hess was missing. Newsmen immediately connected the two and announced to an all but stupefied world that Rudolf Hess, Deputy

Fuehrer of the German Reich, had landed near Glasgow on the night of May 10th by parachute, and was now in secret custody.

The long-suffering people of London had no way of knowing this at the time, but the night bombing of May 10th marked the end of the Luftwaffe's all-out raids on the city.

Between September 7th, 1940, when Alan had seen the first punishing bombing with Maggie, and May 10th, 1941, 24,000 tons of bombs had been dropped on London. Twenty thousand Londoners had been killed outright, and hundreds of thousands more had been hurt. And, of the 58,000 people who lived in Maggie's East End on May 7th, only 16,000 now remained—the rest evacuated or killed.

When his father told him about the casualties in Maggie's district, Alan felt chilled. Then he smiled. Maggie was still there. In answer to a letter he had sent her in charge of the District Warden's office, he had received a postcard showing an emerald and orange sunset over London Bridge and the word, "Cheero," with "Maggie" sprawled untidily over the rest of the space.

To most people's annoyance, the British government, having made him a Prisoner of War, gave out no news about Hess except that he *had* come thinking he could end the war single-handed by negotiation.

Peter arrived home on leave, uncertain whether he'd be able to stay out his "forty-eighter," as no one knew whether the massive air-raids *might* not start up again any moment, and he'd be needed at the squadron. He was a little more sober. Too many of his fighter friends had given their lives to stave the raiders off for him to feel quite as light-hearted about it as he had been at first. Which is not to say that he wasn't gay and perfectly willing to show off the newly won D.F.C. ribbon of which he was so proud.

But David Lyons and Bart remained jittery. "With the slackening of those *very* heavy air attacks on British targets—*if* they have stopped—what does Hitler intend to do next?" Mr. Lyons questioned.

Before the month of June was over, the answer rang out over radios in Washington, Tokyo, London, and transmitters from the Arctic to the tropics.

For several weeks Hitler had been quietly moving his finest air units and troops to the east. On the 22nd of June he threw them into action against his ally, Russia, with every ounce of the explosive fury at their command. A fateful, new war between Germany and Russia began.

The Blitz on Britain was over.

England's war against Germany was far from won yet, and she had by no means seen her last bombs. But in the staunchness with which the people of the British Isles had defied the worst that Hitler could send against them, the tide had already been turned. The long air battle had really been won when the last Nazi bomber headed for home and the fires of London died down on the dawn of May 11th.

When Cicely heard this news, she was sitting in the kitchen shelling peas with Plumey. "You see," Cicely said, "Alan and I knew the Jerries couldn't take England, so that's why we didn't want to go to Oklahoma."

"Well now, that was clever of you," retorted Plumey, "but it'd 'ave saved yer father and mother quite a lot a' trouble if ye'd told us that before ye started fer Glasgow."

"Oh, that," said Cicely. "Then we wouldn't have seen that funny Mr. Hess."

Alan, who was just coming in the back door with Rod, said they'd come to congratulate Dickie.

They'd been down at the firing range watching the Home Guard.

"Did you know, Plumey, that Alf Whitty was accepted in the regular Army yesterday to teach gunnery?" Alan asked.

Plumey dropped her eyes modestly. "That Dickie!" she said. " 'E could teach a kitten to shoot, Dickie could."

Bart Gordon was called home right after the German attack on Russia, and came out to Holmewood for a farewell visit. After dinner the family went out to the terrace for coffee as they had on Gordon's first visit. Again it was a lovely night.

After a short silence Bart burst out, "Y'know, doggone it, I miss Sireen every time I come out here." A murmur of agreement echoed sadly through the fragrant dark.

At that moment an immense white cat with a ridiculous, huge black spot patching one side of its face strolled sociably out from behind the Anderson shelter. After surveying the furniture, it chose a table and in a swift, fluid leap landed on top, wound its fluffy bulk around the coffee tray, gave one paw a lick, and flattened out to sleep.

"*Where* did that animal come from, Cicely—Alan?" their father asked curtly.

"Oh, the cat?" Cicely piped. "Haven't you noticed him before, Daddy? He's been hanging around the house for several days."

There was a great stillness and then, following Bart's lead, everyone broke into a roar of laughter.

"What's her—his name?" Gordon asked, when he could get his breath.

Alan hesitated a moment, but seeing the twinkle in his father's eye, asked:

"What would you think of *Rudolf?*"

About the Authors

CLAYTON KNIGHT was born in Rochester, New York, and grew up just in time to become an airplane pilot in the famed Lafayette Escadrille in World War I. He also served in World War II as an Associated Press special correspondent. His lifelong interest in aviation has earned him many honors and taken him to almost every corner of the earth. It has also provided him with fascinating material for a distinguished list of books and magazine stories that have made him well known both to young people and adults, not only as an author but an artist of uncommon distinction.

Katharine Sturges Knight, co-author of WE WERE THERE AT THE BATTLE OF BRITAIN, has written numerous books with her husband, and also is the author and illustrator of several children's books and magazine articles. Mrs. Knight studied art in the Orient for a year under distinguished Japanese painters after several semesters at the Academy of Fine Arts in Chicago. The Knights have two sons and live in Connecticut.

About the Historical Consultant

THE DUKE OF HAMILTON is highly qualified to review the facts in this book as presented by the authors. A graduate of Eton, and Balliol College, Oxford, Hamilton's own role in the historic unfolding of air strategy in Britain between 1939 and 1945 was a most important one. As a member of the Royal Air Force, he commanded the City of Glasgow Bomber Squadron from 1927 to 1936. When war was declared, he served with the heroic 11th Group, Fighter Command, which bore the full brunt of the early Luftwaffe attacks. Later, he was RAF Sector and Station Commander at Turnhouse, near Edinburgh, and was an unwilling participant in the dramatic affair that began on a moonlit Scottish hillside in May of 1941. The Duke is married and has five sons.

THE "BLITZ" ON LONDON
For 57 nights in the autumn and early winter months
of 1940 the British capital shuddered under a rain
of German high-explosive and fire bombs.